Nuremberg, Mississippi

by Melvin E. Edwards

Praise for *Nuremberg, Mississippi*

"A deeply original examination of justice in America."

Sarah Bird, Acclaimed Novelist,
Author of ***Daughter of a Daughter of a Queen***

"Nuremberg, Mississippi, perfectly captures my own experience of growing up in Jim Crow Mississippi, where Nazi evils shocked us from afar while our own racial evils were so woven into our day-to-day existence that we hardly noticed.

"I highly recommend this eye-opening novel."

Dr. Alan E. Godwin, Psychologist, Author of ***Ties That Blind***

"A compelling look at a horrific time, where an almost-unbeatable opponent avoids the light that tries to reveal it."

"Fast pacing, palpable tension, hard-hitting dialogue, and an evocative setting make Nuremberg, Mississippi, *a must-read."*

Clark Moore, Writer/Editor

"Melvin E. Edwards writes with precision, grace, and a refreshing respect for the power of story to reveal truths we might otherwise miss. Taking his gift for hard questions from podcasting to the page, Edwards asks who we are and where we stand as a country, with keen understanding of history, consequence, and moral nuance. Knowing the weight of words, Nuremberg, Mississippi invites you to slow down, look beyond what's visible, and grapple honestly with distinctions that matter. Written during a key civic moment that will shape our future, this book about our shared history rejects the comfort of easy assumptions and nudges us to ask what is lost when justice is treated as optional rather than essential."

Piper Hendricks, CEO, Stories Change Power

To Charlotte, Joshua, Julian, and Marceile, my grandchildren at the time of its publication. Any future grandchildren can print their names on this page in blue ink.

ACKNOWLEDGMENTS

A very special thanks to my wife, Kim Edwards, for indulging my prolonged bouts with whatever the opposite of writer's block is.

Thank you to attorneys Otto Gallagher, Rick Hall Jr., and Rob Ryan for lending their legal expertise to this project.

Finally, a round of thanks goes to Clark Moore, Andrea Green, and Marty Duren for their meaningful stylistic suggestions. They are truly prose pros.

Table of Contents

PART V
Judgment

PART VI
Aftermath

Publisher's Disclaimer

Nuremberg, Mississippi, is a work of fiction. All characters, institutions, jurisdictions, ordinances, and events portrayed in this novel are fictionalized. Any resemblance to actual persons, living or dead, or to specific governmental bodies, policies, municipalities, or legal proceedings is coincidental and unintentional.

This novel does not depict a single real town, court, or case, nor does it accuse any real person or entity of wrongdoing. Instead, it examines patterns of conduct, institutional behavior, and procedural dynamics that have been documented historically across multiple jurisdictions and time periods. The narrative is constructed to explore how lawful systems can produce predictable harm without relying on overt illegality or individual malice.

Legal procedures, terminology, and documents appearing in this work are presented for narrative purposes only. They are not intended as representations of any specific case, ruling, or legal advice, nor should they be relied upon as such. Where legal mechanisms are depicted, they reflect the logic, customs, and professional norms of the era portrayed, not contemporary standards or interpretations.

The views, actions, and beliefs of the characters do not represent those of the author or publisher.

FOREWORD

At Nuremberg, Chief Prosecutor Robert H. Jackson articulated a principle that would permanently alter international law: that legality does not excuse atrocity, and that crimes committed under color of authority remain crimes, nonetheless. The tribunal rejected obedience, tradition, and national custom as defenses. Civilization, Jackson argued, could not survive their repetition.

Some novels entertain and others interrogate. *Nuremberg, Mississippi* belongs to the second kind. It is less interested in comforting the reader than in awakening moral attention. It asks an old, unnerving question in a distinctly American dialect: What happens when a society learns to call injustice "order," and trains ordinary people to keep it running as routine?

Martin Luther King Jr. warned that the gravest threat is not only open hatred, but the disciplined patience of the "reasonable" – the preference for calm over conscience, for gradualism over truth. In that climate, injustice doesn't need to shout; it only needs to be maintained. Dietrich Bonhoeffer saw how quickly a culture can deform the soul, teaching people to rename cowardice as prudence and complicity as maturity, while offering a religion that blesses the status quo at a safe distance. And Hannah Arendt, watching modern systems at work, named the peril of a world where people stop thinking morally – where harm is administered through procedure, where responsibility shrinks to a job description, and where evil is made sustainable by the ordinary.

You may read *Nuremberg, Mississippi* as more than history. You may read it as an examination – of law, of community, of faith, of the stories we tell ourselves to avoid responsibility. Notice how easily a society can normalize what should appall it – and what it costs to refuse, even quietly, what everyone else calls reasonable.

King called it urgency. Bonhoeffer called it cost. Arendt called it thinking. This book asks what those demands look like when the world offers rewards for compliance – and what it means, in the end, to remain human.

AUTHOR'S NOTE

Nuremberg, Mississippi does not seek to recreate a specific historical event. Its focus is broader – how harm can be delivered through routine professional conduct, and how legality may function as a shield rather than a safeguard.

My own views are strongly influenced by German theologian Dietrich Bonhoeffer, who said moral failure often disguises itself as discipline, professionalism, and obedience. He was talking about the Christian church during the Nazi regime.

The chapters are intentionally brief. That structure reflects the way such systems are experienced – in increments, interruptions, and procedures that appear manageable in isolation. In this sense, the form mirrors the subject.

Only after living with this material for some time did I recognize how familiar many of these patterns were. I grew up with experiences, generational conversations, and silences that taught me how law can shape daily life without ever publicizing itself.

Some rules were written, others enforced, and still others understood without being spoken. This book emerged from that recognition – not from a desire to accuse, but from a need to observe carefully what order permits, and what it requires.

What remains unresolved here is not meaning, but responsibility – what to do with what can be clearly seen. That burden belongs to the reader, as it did to those who lived under these systems, and to those who benefited from them.

The legal documents and terminology appearing in this work were reviewed by three independent attorneys, each licensed in a different state. Some creative elements were retained.

Several surnames appearing in this novel are drawn from my own family history. Names such as Logan, Thorn, Bladen, Jones, Craw, and Bullock come from branches of my ancestry whose lives stretched from Virginia to Texas during the nineteenth century.

Some of these families lived in Leon County, Texas, during the years before and after emancipation, while later generations migrated toward the Gulf Coast. These names are used here as a quiet acknowledgment of those earlier lives that unfolded within the legal and social structures explored in this story.

The characters and events of this novel are entirely fictional. Yet the surnames themselves echo real families whose histories form part of the deeper American landscape from which this book was written.

Nuremberg,
Mississippi

PART I: THE RULES

ONE
Sundown Rules

Tensions rise in sundown towns long before the sun sets. The square begins to empty while the light is still full. Tools are gathered. Conversations just stop mid-sentence. Doors are checked and rechecked.

No announcement is made. The movements advance on expectations alone. By late afternoon, the rules no longer require articulation. They are simply observed.

In Greenville, Mississippi, the law does not announce whom it serves. It makes space for some and withholds it from others. When the sun lowers and the streets are quiet, the courthouse remains lit, guarding a peace that depends on separation and a justice that depends on silence.

When Silas Thorn enters the Myrtle County Courthouse, he does so through the front doors on the north side. The signs that once distinguished those doors have now been removed, but no one in Greenville mistakes their purpose. Men who belong inside before they arrive use them.

The building receives Silas the way his life does – without resistance.

The Negro men who perform the town's manual labor pack up each afternoon from the same grounds where their ancestors were once forced to stay. While the rules governing their departure are unwritten, experience has taught them they are as binding as any statute. What has endured is not the language of the rule, but the certainty of enforcement.

Older residents recall the signs that once marked the town's limits:

NO COLOREDS ALLOWED AFTER DARK

They remember the clarity of the warning and the honesty of its threat. Those signs have since been replaced with more bureaucratic phrasing – **CITY ORDINANCES ENFORCED AT SUNSET** – words arranged to suggest a uniform way these matters were handled rather than exclusion. No one in Greenville pretends that they mean anything different.

The older signs demanded allegiance. The newer ones feign detachment. They allow the town to insist it has changed while preserving the same result. A warning is still issued. A boundary is still drawn. Only the tone has softened, as if Southern manners might redeem cruelty.

Greenville does not preserve its peace by erasing the past, nor by revising its vocabulary. What was once declared openly is now implied, and what is implied is rarely challenged. As the sun begins its descent, the town readies itself, reassured that the rules, even the unspoken ones, will be obeyed.

Greenville, the seat of Myrtle County, is a town of inheritance. In its one-hundred-and-fifty-year history, every mayor has been born within its limits. The North begins somewhere in Tennessee, and anyone beyond it is a Damn Yankee. The town borders on the east by the Cherokee River and on the west by the Davis Estate, a boundary shaped by gerrymandering and sustained pride in its original owner, Jefferson Davis.

The courthouse occupies the center of the square like a civic monument mistaken for a landmark. Its white columns rise as if law itself had assumed an antebellum form. Built before what residents still call the War Between the States and refurbished often enough to appear cared for, it is the one structure no one questions. It is part of the town's identity.

Inside, the air is cool and regulated. Floors are polished. Flags aligned. Portraits of former judges line the walls in dark frames, their expressions solemn and interchangeable. Their names are seldom recalled, but their authority is spoken of with reverence. In Greenville, precedent has less to do with what was decided than with who once sat behind the bench.

Silas Thomas Thorn III didn't grow up knowing he was different. He grew up knowing only that a Thorn was supposed to be something. People told him this through nods, stories, and the subtle burden of expectation placed on a boy who never asked to inherit anything.

His family name had been known in the county long before he was born.

Silas Thorn Sr. – a portrait in the courthouse hallway – had been a man whose spine seemed carved from granite. He fought for land no one else could farm, bought parcels others could not hold, and waged his battles through speeches more than disagreements. He was remembered not for generosity, but for permanence. He died with his boots on, his ledger balanced, and the world still exactly as he preferred it.

Silas Thorn Jr. – his son – perfected the art of being accepted. He smiled when others smiled, voted the way the town needed him to from the State House in Jackson, sat in pews in Greenville with a presence that implied contribution even when he gave very little. His opponents called him "squishy." His friends praised him as "reasonable." No one could quote a single opinion he ever held on his own. That, in its own way, was his triumph.

Silas III learned early that to be a Thorn was to keep the world still and stable.

The name didn't demand brilliance. It demanded restraint. A Thorn didn't innovate; he preserved. He didn't interrupt; he moderated. The family's influence came not from argument, but from predictability. Stability was mistaken for virtue because it spared the town from having to choose.

Silas absorbed this lesson before he understood it. By the time he reached adulthood, compliance felt indistinguishable from character.

The law does not pursue disorder. It waits for it.

A man who remains after sunset is not arrested immediately; instead, he first gets a reminder. Then, he is observed. Only when his presence becomes inconvenient does it become unlawful. Sometimes the final step comes first. Those empowered to enforce it determine the sequence.

City ordinances are drafted deliberately. Words like *race* and *exclusion* never appear. Instead, there are references to public safety, curfew, or loitering – each defensible on its own.

The deputy who enforces these rules understands his role as civic rather than personal. He does not consider himself cruel, even if he is. He considers himself orderly. He tells himself he is preserving norms, honoring tradition, or maintaining balance. When he watches a man leave before dark, he feels satisfaction.

If asked, the mayor would say the laws are applied evenly. The judge would say the ordinances are simply procedural. The clerk would say the paperwork is proper. Each would be speaking honestly, as he understands it. Each would be wrong in precisely the same way.

Silas was born in Greenville in 1926. That fact preceded every other qualification. His name appears in church ledgers, property filings, and council minutes written in careful longhand, and so do his father's and grandfather's. No explanation is required. He belongs.

He pauses beneath the courthouse rotunda out of routine. The building was designed to slow a man, to lend meaning to movement, to make justice appear deliberate. Sound softens here. Every step seems pre-measured.

A deputy stands near the stairwell, at ease.

"Good afternoon, counselor."

"Afternoon."

"Quiet so far."

Silas nods. "Let's keep it that way."

"Yes, sir."

Nothing more is required.

At thirty-eight, Silas dresses as his position demands. Dark suit. Conservative tie. Nothing that makes him unique in this setting. He believes self-control is a discipline and discipline is a form of fairness.

The docket for January 3, 1965, is routine and marks the commencement of the New Year. Ordinance enforcement. Curfew violations. A loitering charge near the east bridge. Nothing exceptional. Nothing that signals consequence.

He removes his coat and places it neatly over the back of his chair. Outside the window, the square has begun its transition. Shadows lengthen. Work concludes.

He checks his watch. Time always matters in Greenville.

The first case is ordinary; a White man charged with public drunkenness and disorderly conduct. Before a defense can be offered, the judge imposes a $10 fine. Nothing more. Nothing less. The gavel falls. The room reconciles back into stillness.

Silas glances toward the window. Three Negro workers are finishing their tasks below. Their movements reflect not only labor, but calculation – how much time remains, how little margin it allows.

He observes them but doesn't comment. They are part of the square's rhythm, present until they are not.

He returns to the docket.

The courthouse remains lit.

As always.

TWO
Bus Stop Justice

Hosea Jones was not represented. That was the first thing Silas noted. No lawyer standing. No whispered conferences. No file passed across a table. Hosea stood where defendants stood when the court didn't expect any resistance.

The charge was municipal — failure to vacate, refusal to comply, repeat violation under a standing order. The clerk read it as routinely as if reading a weather forecast.

Silas watched the judge's face, not the man at the table.

The judge listened with professional detachment, the kind that required no effort because it had long ago become habit. The county's attorney didn't argue. He summarized. Prior citations. A warning was issued and acknowledged. A fine was previously imposed and paid late.

"This is no longer corrective," the attorney said. "It is demonstrative."

That word stayed with Silas.

Hosea spoke only when prompted.

"Yes, sir."

"No, sir."

"I was told."

When asked why he remained after being ordered to leave, Hosea answered plainly.

"I was waiting."

"For what?" the judge asked.

"For the bus," Hosea said.

There was a pause while the court was deciding whether it could matter.

It could not.

The ruling came quickly.

Ninety days in county custody. Maximum fine. Mandatory costs.

And, pursuant to a discretionary provision rarely invoked, suspension of Hosea's eligibility for municipal day labor contracts for eighteen months.

Silas wrote that down.

Eighteen months was bankruptcy.

The judge was deliberate as he explained the decision.

"This court has an obligation to preserve order," the judge said. "When warnings are disregarded, consequences must follow. Otherwise, compliance becomes optional."

Optional.

That was the word Silas circled.

Hosea didn't react. He didn't argue or plead. When the deputies approached, he was resigned to his fate.

The gallery didn't gasp. No one spoke.

The next case was called immediately.

Silas remained seated long enough to see the rhythm reestablish itself. That mattered more than the sentence. The act was taken in stride by the court, causing no disruption.

Outside, in the hallway, Silas caught up with one of the deputies he recognized, a local man who was mid-career. He was the sort of person who truly understood where the boundaries lay.

"Tough sentence," Silas said casually.

The deputy shrugged. "He's been warned."

"For waiting on a bus?"

The deputy smiled slyly. "For not moving when told."

"The permit suspension surprised me."

"That was the point," the deputy said, lowering his voice slightly for effect. "When a man can't work afterward, he remembers."

"Remembers what?"

The deputy considered this, then answered honestly.

"That civic calm matters."

Silas thanked him and stepped outside. Only then did the arithmetic resolve.

The sentence didn't demonstrate excessiveness in any particular aspect. Each component stood within discretion. All of it could be defended.

Silas returned to the courtroom before the benches had fully emptied. Papers were being stacked. The clerk's pen cursived steadily, indifferent to outcome. Another matter would begin shortly. The machinery didn't pause to acknowledge what had passed through it.

Nuremberg, Mississippi

THREE
The Periphery of Safety

Henry Logan learned early to measure time by other people's rules.

Morning belonged to him, work could be done, money earned, and ground covered. The town tolerated production. Men who appeared to be going somewhere were granted more leeway than those who only appeared present.

The laborers sat on the lowered tailgate of the work truck to eat wrapped baloney sandwiches from their metal lunch pails. Sitting in the park would have been more convenient without the NO LOITERING sign. Lunch, lingering, and lurking were not functionally distinguished.

He crossed into the square after sunrise, with toolbox in one hand, and jacket in the other. The silent courthouse rose ahead of him, its steps already swept clean. Someone had been there early, erasing the residue of yesterday. The square depended on that illusion, the suggestion that nothing carried over, that each day stood on its own merits.

Henry noticed these things. He noticed what was erased as deliberately as what was left behind.

Two men were already working near the center of the square. Henry joined them. He recognized the others by face, not by name. They exchanged nods, an established language unto itself. Each knew the expectations of the place – where one could stand, how long one could remain, and when to move on.

Henry kept his pace even. There was nothing defiant in his movement. Defiance was interpreted as rebellion. He had practiced this balance most of his life – present but not provocative, visible but not easily recognized. He understood that the safest posture was competence without assertion.

Entering the courthouse through the south side, the atmosphere shifted. The air cooled. Awareness sharpened. The smell of floor wax and cigarette smoke settled into something nostalgic. A kind of influence was built into the walls themselves.

Silas's office sits at the end of the second-floor corridor. It is modest and personal. Legal pads are stacked. Law books aligned not by sentiment but by use, right next to some of his preferred philosophy authors. He had earned his undergraduate degree in philosophy before moving on to law school.

He looked up when Henry entered, surprised in the way men often were when they forgot who had been keeping their spaces functional.

They exchanged greetings. Politely familiar enough to suggest trust, coolly distant enough to preserve roles. Work was discussed. Things like hinges and wiring. A stair rail that had been repaired once already and required doing properly this time.

The conversation drifted, as it sometimes did, toward books.

Henry cited German theologian Dietrich Bonhoeffer's book *Letters and Papers from Prison* to impress Silas.

He had read parts of the work, borrowed from a man who kept books the way others kept tools.

Henry didn't explain why that book mattered to him. He had learned these things invited judgment, and judgment was rarely unaligned.

"Bonhoeffer is a challenge," Silas said.

"Yes," Henry replied. "And so is living without asking why things are the way they are."

Henry continued chatting while he adjusted the hinge once more, checking the alignment by feel rather than sight.

"Have you ever heard of James Baldwin? He writes about what happens when a country mistakes order for morality."

He didn't name the book and didn't look up. The thought was offered the way one offers a fact already established, not as an argument seeking response.

Silas studied the ceiling, then the window.

"He's angry," Silas said finally. "I understand why, but anger doesn't build coalitions."

Henry's jaw clenched as he replayed "Angry" in his mind. He had learned over the years that Negro men were considered militant and, therefore, dangerous. He was neither militant nor angry.

Henry tightened the final screw. The hinge no longer resisted. "Maybe not," he said. "But neither does pretending things are orderly when they're only controlled."

Silas didn't answer that. Silence, too, is a form of self-discipline.

Later, as Henry gathered his tools, he said quietly, "I was outside when Hosea's case was called."

Silas didn't hesitate. "He knew the rules."

Henry waited, but the words didn't change.

He left without an argument.

Though the sentence was plainly spoken, it hovered over the room like Gulf Coast fog.

On Wednesday nights, Henry's wife took the children, Daniel and Caroline, to Bible study. She dressed them carefully, checked their shoes, and gathered the coloring books that kept them distracted and occupied. Faith, for her, was communal – something practiced aloud, in sequence, among others who believed the same things. It offered structure and assurance, but especially hope.

Henry stayed home. He didn't object to her attending church. His faith was quieter. It lived in the detail to actions rather than institutional attendance.

Once the house settled, he put a record on the record player and listened without moving. These were his only private moments all week. He put on Ray Charles first, then Smokey Robinson. He didn't play them loudly. He listened the way he did everything else – with attention and with self-awareness.

The music altered time without suspending it. For an hour, sometimes less, his world loosened its grip. Enough to breathe, though nothing had materially changed.

Later that week, Henry arrived at Silas's house to begin the work they had discussed.

The house sat within the most comfortable edge of Greenville. Close enough to belong. Far enough to require attention to timing. Silas's to-do list mentioned a step that needed reinforcing, and some wiring done years earlier that required patience to correct. Silas hovered, then retreated. The conversation that Silas initiated filled the pauses.

Bonhoeffer again. Obedience, delay, responsibility. Whether restraint was a virtue or merely a habit elevated into principle.

Henry was enjoying the conversation so much that he let his guard down. In his world, that could be a subtle movement with a devastating impact. The daylight had already faded.

By the time he stepped outside, the margin had skimmed to almost nothing.

He drove carefully. Too carefully invited notice. Not carefully enough invited worse. He chose the middle, as he always did.

For a moment, he wondered whether leaving earlier next time would solve anything at all. The thought embarrassed him, and he dismissed it before it could harden into hope.

The red and blue beacons appeared before he could decide which choice had betrayed him.

The stop didn't feel sudden. It felt scheduled.

The lights appeared behind Henry as he reached the stretch of road where movement narrowed and explanation rarely helped. He pulled over immediately. The engine remained on as the deputy approached with a lowered hat and a deliberate, composed manner.

"I know you know the ordinance," the deputy said, answering the question he had not even asked.

Henry didn't say whose house he had been working in. He didn't mention the hinge that had taken longer than expected, or the sunlight that had shifted while no one was watching. The ordinance was not interested in sequence.

The deputy spoke in the language of process, time, location, and citation number. No accusation or raised voice. When Henry was asked to step out of the car, he did so cautiously, placing his hands where they were expected before he was told.

By the time they reached the courthouse, the lights were already on.

Silas arrived before the paperwork was finished.

He moved quickly, his voice low, measured, already translating the situation into terms that could be managed. He apologized to Henry without naming the offense, offered representation without hesitation, and framed the incident as an unfortunate miscalculation rather than a violation.

In the courtroom the following morning, Henry stood exactly where he was directed. The charge was read as written – facially indifferent, precise, and stripped of motive. Silas listened closely, noting Henry's posture: upright, attentive, and nonreactive.

When sentencing was announced – 90 days – Silas didn't object immediately. He waited because timing mattered.

He spoke of employment. Of reliability. Of cooperation. He described Henry as stable, capable, and a native Mississippian. He didn't challenge the ordinance directly. He appealed instead to discretion.

"He's one of the good ones, Your Honor."

The judge listened without expression.

After a pause long enough to suggest consideration, the sentence was reduced to 30 days.

The clerk entered the revision cleanly into the record.

Silas felt a sense of relief. Thirty days was not nothing, but it was less than ninety. It was restraint exercised responsibly.

He gathered his papers, already placing the matter behind him. The docket moved on. The courtroom exhaled.

Henry didn't look back.

By the time the door closed, Silas had convinced himself the law had listened.

Later that afternoon, Silas stopped outside the clerk's office while a federal deputy walked by in the corridor, carrying a briefcase and appearing preoccupied.

"Busy day," Silas offered.

The deputy nodded without stopping.

"We're tracking a few towns," he said. "Nothing personal. Just patterns."

Silas waited for clarification that didn't arrive.

"What happens when you find one?" he asked.

The deputy stopped then, only briefly.

"Usually nothing," he said. "At first."

Silas frowned.

"And after?"

The deputy considered the question with mild curiosity, surprised anyone would ask.

"After," he said, "the people who made themselves visible usually regret it."

He adjusted the strap of his briefcase and continued down the hall.

Silas stood alone, unsure why the word "usually" bothered him more than anything else.

Nuremberg, Mississippi

THREE AND ONE-FOURTH
Bureaucracy

The square never publicly announced when a man had stayed too long.

Henry finished his work earlier than expected. The deputy passed once, then again. Nothing was said. In the daytime, the town preferred patience.

Henry left just early enough. That fact appeared nowhere.

What followed did.

Forms that once moved quickly now required additional signatures. A clerk who had always used Henry's name switched to his file number. The changes were small and defensible. None violated policy, and that was the point.

At home, Helen inventoried what remained. She didn't ask questions that required explanation. She noted what they would need to stretch and what could not break again this month.

Henry had started viewing the upcoming summer as a buffer — a breathing space.

He already had three small, routine contracts lined up well in advance. Provided everything unfolded smoothly, he wouldn't have to take on any additional work until September.

No new clients, and no unfamiliar journeys.

He never voiced these thoughts, not even to Helen, because hope wasn't something he liked to acknowledge openly. Yet, he caught himself counting by weeks instead of days, picturing evenings free from endless calculations.

He just wanted one season where nothing needed to be justified.

Across town, Silas closed a file he believed finished.

The sentence had been reduced. The court had responded. From his vantage point, restraint had worked. The system had corrected itself. That belief resolved comfortably.

Two days later, Henry received the federal letter from the district court.

It didn't accuse. It was an invitation.

Later that month came the federal interview. Henry arrived early and took the third chair from the end. Each interview lasted six to eight minutes.

When his name was called, he stood immediately.

The questions were chronological. Time. Location. Sentence. Reduction. Compliance. The pen moved steadily.

"You applied for a municipal permit following release."

"Yes."

"Status?"

"Suspended."

"Pending review?"

"Yes."

The pen stopped.

"Did you comply with the relocation notice?"

"No."

The man looked up.

"This interview is administrative," he said. "Not disciplinary."

Henry understood.

One final question was asked.

"When you remained after sunset, did you believe you were permitted to do so under existing ordinance?"

"Yes," Henry said. "For a time."

The pen moved again.

Outside, the light was sharper than expected. A patrol car idled at the corner. Nothing happened.

Two days later, a memo circulated.

It summarized trends, praised consistency, and recommended continuing monitoring.

No intervention warranted at this time.

The record didn't accuse.

Silas heard of the review in passing. Routine. Nothing unusual.

Still, Henry came to mind.

That night, Silas opened the book he had once dismissed as angry and read it more methodically than before.

The next morning, while reviewing the docket, he noticed the entry.

Logan, Henry.

One arrest. One conviction. Sentence reduced. Time served.

The notation didn't stand out in any significant way.

What the record didn't show was how easily a closed file could still be informally opened against him, through inspections and delays. Through discretion exercised elsewhere. Henry had satisfied his legal debt, but not his new unpayable deficit to the town.

Tomorrow, Henry would knock on Silas Thorn's door.

Not to ask for mercy.

To insist the record remain open.

Nuremberg, Mississippi

- 22 -

THREE AND ONE-HALF
No Voices Raised

Henry didn't raise his voice. He stood with hands folded, posture careful, and expression unreadable, as if attending to a transaction already decided.

"Mr. Logan," the clerk said, "you've been advised."

"I understand," Henry replied.

"You've been given an alternative."

"I was."

"And you're declining it."

"Yes, sir."

The alternative was simple; sign the acknowledgment and agree to the proposed time frame for relocation. Reapply later under the revised ordinance. Everyone in the room understood what that meant: delay, dilution, or disappearance. Or all three.

Henry had listened to it all without interrupting.

"I'm not asking for an exception," he said. "I'm asking for what's already written."

"Sir," the clerk said carefully, "the procedure allows discretion."

"I know," Henry said. "That's why I'm here."

There it was.

Not defiance in tone. Defiance in framing. Henry was not resisting authority. He was insisting that it mean what it said.

The supervisor finally spoke.

"Mr. Logan, you're making this harder than it needs to be."

Henry looked him right in his eyes. "No, sir. I'm making it exact."

The supervisor exhaled forcefully. He reached for the file and flipped it closed.

"Then we proceed formally."

That phrase cost Henry more than anything that followed.

Formal meant referral. The term "Formal" referred to a review process. Once formality was introduced, matters that could previously be resolved discreetly now demanded uniformity and adherence to established procedures.

The notice arrived three days later.

Permit suspended pending compliance review.

Operations prohibited during the review period.

Violations subject to enforcement.

The language didn't accuse Henry of wrongdoing; it simply removed the conditions that made his livelihood possible.

Henry lost the contract first. Then the equipment access. Then, the informal credit arrangement that had never existed on paper and therefore could not be defended.

The tasks remained present, albeit in a different form.

The primary change was the sequence of operations.

Morning assignments were delayed, routes became less direct with added detours, and tasks were rescheduled or modified rather than canceled.

At this point, Henry ceased tracking the number of weeks that had elapsed.

He had grown up watching it happen. Still, he didn't sign.

When Silas asked him later – carefully, almost clinically – whether it had been worth it, Henry didn't answer right away.

They were sitting at the small table by the window. The afternoon light cut across the room, illuminating dust on the sill that no one ever cleaned because it never quite felt like dirt.

"They wanted me to move so they wouldn't have to explain," Henry said finally. "I stayed so they'd have to."

"And now?"

Henry smiled, but there was no humor in it.

"Now they don't explain," he said. "They make sure they don't allow."

Silas said nothing.

Henry reclined, aware of the void where his daily routine once weighed on him.

Work had always offered order, and so did hardship. Now, he was experiencing something completely different.

"They'll say I chose this," Henry continued. "That I was stubborn and uncooperative."

"Did you?" Silas asked.

Henry considered the question.

"No. I chose not to disappear quietly," he said.

The cost was not jail this time. It was thinner and sharper.

Henry had seen this lesson taught before.

This time, it had been addressed to him.

THREE AND THREE-FOURTHS
The Courtesy

The young woman at the counter was new. She called everyone by their last name on first reference, then Sweety and Sugar thereafter.

Henry noticed her immediately because she looked up when he approached. That alone set her apart. Most clerks had learned to keep their eyes on the forms until the exchange was complete.

She was not there the last time he sought a status update. She couldn't be more than 20, so she was likely a summer-only hire. Light brown hair set in a single ponytail and a pencil tucked behind her ear instead of resting where it belonged. Her desk was slightly out of order in a functional manner.

"Good morning," she said.

"Morning."

He slid the permit inquiry across the counter. He had filled it out methodically, block letters, nothing crossed out. He had learned that strikethroughs invited questions.

She took the form and read it all the way through. Not skimmed, actually read.

That, too, was new.

"Mr. Logan," she said, glancing up again. "You're checking on the status?"

"Yes, ma'am."

She nodded, then pulled the file drawer open farther than most people would, despite its resistance.

"Just a moment," she said.

Henry waited.

The room was quiet in a governmental bureaucracy kind of way – papers shifting, a distant phone ringing unanswered, and footsteps somewhere behind a door that never fully closed.

She found the file.

She was surprised by the sheer administrative weight. Henry noticed a change in her posture as she methodically flipped through the pages.

He braced himself.

Pending review.

Suspended.

Further notice.

Instead, she hesitated.

"I'm not supposed to say this," she said, lowering her voice, making it barely noticeable. "But your paperwork is... complete."

Henry said nothing.

"There's nothing missing," she continued. "No errors. No outstanding fees. No additional compliance listed."

She turned the page back and forth once more, looking for something that might justify the pause she felt.

"I don't understand why it's still marked this way," she said.

Again, Henry waited.

She looked up at him again. Really looked this time.

"Sweety," she said, choosing her words carefully, "it's all in order."

For a moment, Henry allowed himself to imagine what it might mean if order worked in his favor.

He didn't smile. He didn't thank her yet. He had learned better.

"I was told it required review," he said.

"Yes," she replied quickly. "That's what it says. But reviews usually move faster than this."

Henry tapped his foot rhythmically.

She noticed then how anxious he looked, and it flustered her because it felt misplaced.

"Is something wrong, Sugar?"

The question landed gently. Almost kindly.

Henry thought about it.

"I've been here three times trying to get these permits," he admitted. "I need to get back to work."

She smiled just enough to register intention.

"I'll be right back."

When she disappeared through the door behind the counter, his hopes faded.

The clock above the filing cabinets ticked loudly, marking time like a bomb's countdown.

A minute passed.

Then two.

Then three.

When she returned, her expression was unchanged. She was holding his paperwork.

"Take this and don't tell anyone who did this," she whispered.

"Of course."

The paper was folded in half. The ink faint.

"Thank you," he said.

She watched him as he turned to leave.

She called after him softly, careful not to carry as he reached the door.

"Good luck, Sweety."

Henry halted, but didn't turn around.

"God bless you."

Outside, he unfolded the document.

Under Active Review. Provisional license granted.

Henry received a letter from the county a week later, but the supervisor had denied the permit.

He heard through the grapevine that the young woman had been fired.

PART II: VISIBILITY

FOUR
A Question of Representation

The sound of inevitability was one that Silas recognized by heart.

It was not loud, and it didn't broadcast its entrance. It arrived the way the weather did – in the way the air shifted, the way the texture of a room seemed already pre-arranged for what was about to happen.

Henry chose not to make an advance phone call. To him, that was knocking, even asking permission to be heard. He decided to steel his courage without announcing himself.

While seated in the chair opposite Silas's desk, he rested his hands calmly in his lap. He had removed his hat and set it on his knees, and didn't look around the office. He had been there before – twice technically – but this was different. Before, he had come as a worker and as a defendant. Now he had come as something less familiar.

Silas closed the file he had been reading.

"What did your father want to do," he said, "after the Army?"

Like Henry, that question didn't RSVP before arriving.

"Wanted to do?" he said, clarifying.

Silas affirmed. "Yes, after the war."

Henry considered this for a minute because no one had ever asked him.

"He talked about owning something," Henry said, finally. "Didn't much matter what. A repair shop. A feed store. Something with his name, J.L. Logan, on the door."

Silas listened intently.

"He had a knack with engines," Henry went on. "Could take a thing apart and put it back together better than he found it. Folks noticed. White folks, too."

"And?"

The memory confused Henry, and he smiled with pent-up emotion in his eye.

"And the loans never came. The zoning never worked. The war ended, but the rules didn't."

Silas lowered his eyes to the file in front of him, though he didn't open it.

"So he went back to work," Silas said.

"Yeah, for people who'd never had to explain why they were the only ones who deserved to own anything."

Silas quietly absorbed this. After a moment, he said, "Did he talk about it later?"

Henry shook his head. "No. He talked about me."

That rested between them, solid and complete.

"Thank you," Silas said, as a solemn recognition.

Henry lifted his head, as if the exchange had concluded exactly where it was meant to.

"You didn't call," Silas said.

"No."

There was no apology in it. A simple confirmation.

Silas leaned back, testing how much the chair would bend. As always, the springs protested with a familiar squeak. He had intended to oil them, just as he'd planned to repair several other things.

"I don't usually take meetings without an appointment."

"I know. I won't take long."

That, Silas thought, was not a promise. It was a measurement.

Silas waited because he had learned, over the years, that silence was often more instructive than questions. Judges used it. Clerks used it. He had used it himself when he wanted a man to understand that the room didn't belong to him.

Henry sat without shifting.

Finally, Silas said, "How are you?"

Henry evaluated the question thoroughly, analyzing it from several perspectives before proceeding.

"I'm working," he said. "My wife is well. The children are growing faster than I can keep track of."

These were answers that required no response.

"And the work?" Silas asked.

"It's steady for now," Henry said. "As steady as it can be."

Silas glanced down at the desk. His nameplate sat where it always had: Silas T. Thorn III, Attorney-at-Law. His parents gave it to him when he finished law school at Vanderbilt. Everything was in its place.

He said, "You didn't come here to talk about carpentry."

"No," Henry said.

A declaration by way of a simple subtraction.

As Silas twiddled his thumbs, he felt a faint, irritating tremor in his bum knee.

"What is it you want from me, Henry?" Silas asked.

Henry lifted his eyes, making direct eye contact with Silas.

"I want you to represent me," he said.

The words sat between them and didn't move.

Silas felt something close in his chest – not panic, or anger. Only mild confusion.

"I don't think that's a good idea," Silas said.

Henry seemed to have expected this.

"I figured you might say that."

Silas stood and moved toward the window. Outside, the square was quieter than it would be later. Two men spoke in low voices beside a parked pickup truck. A haberdashery loomed across the street, its fresh white paint catching the sunlight.

"You've already had me as your counsel," Silas said, his back still turned. "And you know how that turned out."

"Yes," Henry said.

The word hung heavy. It was not an accusation. It proved to be an accounting.

Silas said, "I can recommend someone."

Henry didn't respond.

Silas turned back. "There are lawyers in Jackson and in New Orleans. Men who specialize in this."

"I'm not looking for a specialist," Henry said.

Silas stopped short of his chair.

"No," Henry continued. "I'm looking for someone who understands what happened."

Silas felt the sentence land precisely where it had been aimed.

"I understood the law," Silas said. "That was the problem."

Henry didn't argue. He shifted slightly in the chair, crossing one ankle over the other.

"You told me once that the law doesn't always move fast, but it remembers."

"I don't recall saying that."

"You did," Henry said. "It was after the sentencing."

That day returned with unwelcome clarity: the humid courtroom, the judge's dignified, impersonal voice, the sentence delivered as if measured by a scale rather than a man. Three months in county jail. It was all lawful, defensible, and entirely predictable.

Henry had not reacted. That had been the worst part. No protest, no visible anger. A tightening around the eyes, knowing he had expected no other outcome and was disappointed only in himself for hoping otherwise.

Silas said, "I did what I could."

Henry's voice remained even. "I know."

The words didn't absolve him. They did something worse – they acknowledged competence without forgiveness.

Silas returned to his chair and sat.

"What you're asking," Silas said slowly, "is not simple. You're talking about a lawsuit against the State.

"Not the county. Not the town. The State of Mississippi. The Confederacy has a permanent residence here."

"Yes," Henry said. "And the case could go all the way to the Supreme Court. The Feds are already looking into patterns established around here. We can help nudge the case along."

Silas exhaled. "That kind of case does not make friends."

Henry allowed himself the faintest hint of a smile. "I don't have many of those left."

Silas looked at him sharply, then away.

"And you think I do?" Silas asked.

Henry didn't answer immediately. When he did, his voice was quiet.

"I think you already lost the ones that used to matter," he said. "Same as me."

Silas felt the truth of it come down uncomfortably. He had not been invited to dinner in weeks. Conversations stopped when he entered a room. His name still carried weight, but it had lost its edge.

"Why me?" Silas asked. "Why now?"

Henry leaned forward slightly, resting his forearms on his thighs.

"Because you were there," he said. "And because you know what it costs when the law decides it's done enough, and I'm tired of waiting for things to change. Transitions sometimes need a little nudge."

Silas felt the old familiar instinct rise – the urge to explain, to contextualize, to defend the machinery that had shaped him.

"I can't undo what happened," Silas said.

"I'm not asking you to," Henry replied.

The simplicity of it was disarming.

"I served the time," Henry went on. "I did what the court required. I came home. I went back to work. Nothing about that changed the rule. It only confirmed it."

Silas said nothing.

"I'm not asking you to feel better," Henry said. "I'm asking you to help me make it visible."

Silas stared at the desk and the shelf of law books, the systematic tools of his trade.

"And if we lose?" Silas asked.

Henry shrugged. "Then it will be written down that we tried."

Silas felt a tightening in his throat.

"And if we win?" he asked.

Henry gave it some thought.

"Then they'll say it was never personal," he said. "That it was always procedure. I'm prepared for that."

"You understand," Silas said, slowly, "that this will follow you."

"It already does."

Silas closed his eyes. Beneath it all, the question he had never been able to answer for himself lingered: what responsibility a man had when he obeyed rules he knew were wrong.

Henry stood.

"I've said what I came to say," he said.

Silas looked up. "You're certain?"

"Yes."

Silas hesitated, then spoke.

"If I do this," he said, "it won't fix what I broke."

Henry placed his hat back on his head.

"I know," he said. "But it might keep it from breaking someone else."

Henry moved toward the door. His hand rested briefly on the knob.

"Mr. Thorn," he said.

Silas looked up.

"The case name," Henry said. "It should be mine."

Silas swallowed.

"Of course," he said.

After Henry left, Silas remained seated. The office felt smaller now, as if the center had shifted.

He reached for a blank sheet of paper and wrote the caption slowly, as if each word were heavier than the ink.

Logan v. Mississippi

He stared at the paper before placing it in the drawer, but he didn't yet understand that the decision had already begun to cost him.

Nuremberg, Mississippi

FOUR AND ONE-HALF
The Shift

At first, the changes appeared only at the edges – an extra pause, a sentence that arrived intact but slightly misaligned, its form shifting before reaching him. Henry returned the following week with the same paperwork he had brought every other time. It was unchanged. He had checked it the night before, again that morning, and once more in the truck before walking inside.

The clerk didn't look up immediately. That was not unusual.

What was new was the file.

It was already on the counter when the clerk finally met Henry's eyes.

"Mr. Logan," the clerk said.

Henry nodded.

The clerk opened the folder, glanced at the top page, then closed it again.

"You're still listed as active," he said.

Henry waited.

"There's been a notation."

The clerk slid the folder slightly to one side, keeping his hand on it.

"Just procedural," he added. "Nothing adverse."

Henry folded his arms.

"What kind of notation?" he asked.

The clerk hesitated – briefly, but deliberately.

"Additional review."

"Additional to what?"

"The usual."

Henry nodded.

"Does it require anything from me?"

"No," the clerk said. "You've done everything correctly."

The sentence stopped there.

"This may take some time," the clerk added.

"How much?" Henry asked.

The clerk smiled, uncertain.

"We don't usually measure it that way."

Henry let that pass.

"When did the notation appear?" he asked.

The clerk looked down again.

"Recently."

"After my last visit?"

A pause.

"Yes."

Henry nodded once.

The clerk closed the folder and slid it back across the counter.

As Henry turned to leave, the clerk spoke again.

"You're not in trouble."

Henry stopped.

"I didn't think I was," he said.

Outside, the day was ordinary. Nothing had been denied. Nothing had been taken.

But the process no longer waited for Henry to appear. It adjusted in advance, like his compliance had become a known quantity rather than a qualifying one.

By the time Henry reached his driveway, the change was complete.

In fact, it named him, and others like him.

He lingered in the driveway before entering the quiet house. The kids were still out, and Helen was at the store. He checked the time, and he was done earlier than usual.

He realized, almost matter-of-factly, that life wouldn't return to its previous rhythm, even if things resumed as before. Mornings would no longer be his. The town had adapted to him. His work remained, but his freedom – the margin – was gone, and only now did he see how vital it was.

Henry went inside. When Helen later asked about his day, he simply replied, "Nothing happened." She understood.

FIVE
Inside the House

When Silas parked a half block from the Logans' house, he told himself it was because the street was narrow. Because the curb dipped unevenly. Because habit had taught him not to block driveways or mailboxes. None of these explanations satisfied him.

The truth was simpler. He had never done this before.

He sat in the car, engine running, and the radio off. The house ahead was modest and well-kept, its paint recently refreshed, the porch swept clean. Nothing flashy. The place didn't draw attention to itself.

Silas adjusted his tie, then loosened it again. He removed his jacket and folded it over his arm before stepping out of the car.

Henry met him at the door.

"Mr. Thorn," Henry said.

"Henry."

There was a brief, awkward pause before Henry stepped aside to let him in.

The air inside the house was cooler than Silas expected. The fan and cross breeze worked wonders before summer hit. The room was tidy without feeling staged. Furniture arranged for utility rather than impression. A dining table sat beyond the entry, its surface mostly clear.

Mostly.

Silas observed that the house drew very little attention to itself; it seemed content to remain unnoticed. The walls didn't display accomplishment. The shelves contained a few books. What stood out instead was stability – objects kept because they worked, not because they impressed anyone.

It struck him that this restraint mirrored the way Henry moved through public spaces: present, precise, unprovocative. The same economy governed both.

Silas noticed the paperback book on the dining table and took note of it to address later.

It lay near the center of the table, thin and well-worn, with dog-eared pages and edges beginning to tatter. The cover was plain. No flourish. Like the house, it did not attempt charm.

The 1964 Negro Motorist Green Book.

Henry saw him looking.

"We were just talking," Henry said, nodding toward the table. "You can sit, if you'd like."

Silas moved slowly, careful not to disturb something fragile, though nothing in the room suggested fragility. He set his jacket over the back of a chair and sat opposite Henry.

Silas had expected discomfort, an unfamiliar chair, a sense of intrusion, and the awareness that his presence altered the neighborhood. What he had not expected was ease.

The house was tranquil. Neither vacant nor tentative. Simply serene.

What struck him was how rarely he'd been required to account for calm. Here, it felt earned.

The floorboards remained silent beneath his footsteps. The air smelled faintly of something warm that had been cooked earlier and put away properly. Nothing here was temporary.

Henry was seated opposite him at the compact kitchen table, posture relaxed. Not deferential, simply at rest in the one place that rest was recognized.

Silas noticed details without meaning to. The careful repair along the window frame. A stack of mail squared neatly beside the wall, already opened, already sorted. A pencil was strategically placed on top of the stack. The room bore the marks of repetition – things done the same way, every day, because the day required them.

"This is a nice place," Silas said finally.

"It's home."

They sat for a moment longer. The percolator behind them clicked softly as it cooled.

Silas became aware, with mild surprise, that he had not yet mentioned the law. In his office, it arrived immediately. Here, it felt intrusive.

Silas had asked his questions already – the ones that justified the visit. He had explained timelines and risks, and phrased deliberately enough to sound impartial. Henry had listened, asked for one clarification, and said he understood.

What came next had not.

Silas reclined slightly in his chair, then stopped himself, unsure whether the movement implied too much familiarity. He sat upright.

"Henry," he said, pausing. "Can I ask you something not related to the case?"

Henry established direct eye contact. "You already have."

It almost drew a smile, almost.

"You're… articulate," Silas said, immediately dissatisfied with the word. He corrected himself. "You're very smart. You comprehend the law faster than some men who went to school for it."

Henry waited for what would come next.

Silas eventually understood that he had been addressing a concept previously unnamed to him: access. Throughout his life, he had erroneously equated fluency with authorization.

Silas cleared his throat. "I suppose what I'm asking is, why didn't you ever go to college?"

The question was asked gently, causing no noticeable reaction in the room.

Henry looked down at his hands. Answering the question required a chronological explanation.

"As I was explaining in your office, my father came back from the war in '46 when I was nine years old," he said. "Honorably discharged."

His voice was flat, instructional. "He had paperwork, discharge papers, letters, and everything they told him to keep."

Silas nodded reflexively. He knew the outline of this story. At least, he thought he did.

"He was told he could use the GI Bill," Henry continued. "School, training, loans, all that. The same list everyone else got."

Henry reached for the pencil on the table and turned it a couple of times between his fingers.

"But when he went to apply," he said, "the schools wouldn't take him. Said they were full. Or said they didn't offer the right programs. Or said nothing at all."

Silas felt his jaw tighten, though he didn't yet understand why.

"The benefits didn't disappear," Henry went on.

"They just… didn't land anywhere. Banks wouldn't process the loans. Colleges wouldn't process the enrollment. The bill existed. The access didn't."

Silas inhaled, slow and shallow.

"So my father worked," Henry said. "He worked the way men do when they're told they've been given something they can't touch. He used what he could. He bought tools. He taught himself. He taught me."

He looked up then.

"When it was my turn," Henry said, "it wasn't even a question. We already knew how the system worked. You don't apply for things that were never meant for you. I even graduated a year early at the top of my class."

The words were not bitter. They were simply stated as fact.

Silas stared at the table. At the grain of the wood, and the small scar near the edge where something sharp had once slipped and partially embedded itself.

"But you did everything right," he said, before he could stop himself.

Henry's brow furrowed subtly, reflecting a sense of mild confusion rather than offense.

"Yes," he said.

The simplicity of the answer broke something.

Before Silas could make sense of it, an unexpected warmth flooded his eyes, a sensation he hadn't experienced since long before he learned the value of exaggerated self-control. Almost reflexively, he turned his head away, as if searching the wall for a way out.

"I'm sorry," he said, though he was no longer certain what the apology was for.

Henry didn't speak. He didn't fill the space.

Silas pressed his right thumb hard against the side of his knee, grounding himself in the small, familiar pain. His breath came unevenly now to his own surprise.

"My family," he said, and stopped.

"We were told the rules," Silas continued, counting to three on his right fingers, "Service. Education. Patience. We were taught that if you did the correct things in the correct order, the outcome was… predictable, almost guaranteed."

His voice failed him briefly.

"And you're telling me," he said, "that the order was never the point."

Henry regarded him, not as an attorney or opponent, but as a person faced with a reality too overwhelming to grasp all at once.

"I'm telling you," Henry said, "that the order was enforced. It's the access that was never within reach."

Silas covered his mouth with his hand. He didn't sob, but the composure he had worn so methodically or so long slipped enough to be visible.

Henry's wife, Helen, had entered quietly from the kitchen. She brought out two glasses of water, then remained standing.

Henry felt tears welling up in his own eyes, then took a sip from the water glass his wife had given him.

Silas lowered his hand.

"I didn't know," he said.

Henry nodded again, the same small motion as before.

"That's not unusual."

The percolator was cold now.

The handbook remaining between them seemed like a direction to distract his emotions temporarily.

"I didn't know these were still in print," Silas said with an embarrassed smile.

"I'm surprised you've even heard of it," Henry responded.

"I went to law school in Nashville, and I overheard a couple of Negro men discussing it at the bus stop. That was probably 15 years ago."

"They update them every year," Helen said. "Roads change. Places close."

Silas paused, unsure what reply was required.

Henry said, "It's easier than guessing."

Silas reached for the book without thinking, then stopped himself.

"May I?" he asked.

Henry gave the okay.

Silas picked it up. The pages were thin and densely printed. Cities are listed in careful columns. Hotels, gas stations, cafés, barber shops, even churches. Places where a man could stop without explanation. Most importantly, without intimidation.

"It reads like a map," Silas said.

Helen gave a small, humorless smile. "It's a warning system and a safety net."

Silas turned a page, then another.

"What if you forgot it?"

The question came out before he had fully considered it.

Henry answered first. "We don't."

Silas looked up.

Helen said, "It stays by the door when we're traveling. If we leave without it, we turn around."

Silas closed the book partway.

"Even if you're only going a few hours?"

"Especially then," Helen replied.

Silas frowned slightly.

"And if you didn't?" he pressed. "If you stopped somewhere by mistake. A restaurant, say. One that wasn't in a sundown town."

"The sign wouldn't say it," Henry said. "Not anymore."

"You'd know," Helen said. "Before you sat down."

"How?" Silas asked.

Helen paused, then answered like she was listing titles on a bookshelf.

"The way the room goes quiet. The way someone stops smiling. The way a waitress takes too long to come back, or comes back too fast."

Silas pulled back.

"And if you stayed?"

Henry's voice was calm. "Then we'd be asked to leave."

"And if you didn't?" Silas said.

Helen looked him in the eye. "Then it would depend on the time."

Silas felt his stomach tighten.

"The later it is," Henry said, "the fewer words there are."

Silas looked down at the book again.

"So, this," he said, tapping the cover lightly, "keeps you from having to test that."

"Yes," Helen said.

Silas set the handbook back on the table carefully.

"And how do you prepare?" he asked her. "For a long trip."

Helen sat at last, wiping her hands on her pale-yellow apron.

"I pack food," she said. "Sandwiches that don't need refrigeration. Fruit that won't bruise. I pack water."

Silas nodded.

"I make sure the children use the bathroom before we leave," she continued. "Every time we stop. Even if they say they don't need to."

Silas shifted in his chair.

"I pack extra clothes," Helen said. "For accidents...or delays."

"What kind of delays?" Silas asked.

Helen looked at him. "Sometimes you don't stop where you planned."

Silas felt the heavy meaning of it.

"I make sure he checks the car twice," she said. "Gas. Tires. Lights. I don't like giving anyone a reason to pull us over."

Silas's jaw tightened.

"And the route?"

Henry answered. "We don't take the shortest one. There's no Route 66 for us in Mississippi, or anywhere else."

Silas let out a breath he hadn't realized he was holding.

"The State will say none of this is required," Silas said quietly.

"That's why it works. That's the way I see it anyway."

Silas leaned forward, elbows on the table.

"And you want this understood," he said, "even if it isn't entered into the record."

Helen was positive. "Especially if it's not entered into the record."

Silas sat back.

"I've driven this state my whole life," he said. "I've never planned a trip this way."

Henry looked at him seriously. "We plan so we can arrive."

Silas nodded slowly.

"I've never been inside a Negro home before," he said.

Helen didn't correct him. She didn't smile.

"You're in one now," she said.

Silas stood.

"I'll take the case."

Again, there was no handshake.

Silas didn't reach for his jacket right away.

He remained standing near the table, looking not at the book now but at the ordinary objects around it, the empty glass, and the faint ring where moisture had settled and dried. Evidence of life that proceeded carefully.

"There's something else," Silas said.

Henry looked up.

Silas chose his words with care.

"This case won't stay in the courtroom," he said. "Regardless of how it ends."

Henry was stopped cold. "What do you mean?"

"It will trouble people," Silas continued, "because it names things they prefer remain unspoken."

Helen didn't interrupt. She had gone still, her hands folded in her lap.

"And when people feel exposed," Silas said, "they look for ways to lash out."

Henry said, "You mean punish us, right?"

"Yes."

The word rested simply in the space between them.

"The law will pretend detachment," Silas said. "But outside of it, there are no transcripts. No objections and no record."

"It won't be you," Henry said.

"I didn't say ..."

"It won't be you," Henry repeated, gently. "Not the way it will be me."

Silas felt the truth of it resolve, sharp and unavoidable.

"They won't call it retaliation," Helen said quietly. "It's their way of keeping us in 'our place,' and you'll be called names you've never been called before because of us."

Silas turned toward her.

"They'll call it a coincidence," she went on. "A job that doesn't come through. A truck that won't stop when it should. A warning given too late to matter."

"I can try to prepare for that," he said. "There are motions we can file. Requests for protection."

Henry shook his head.

"That would make it worse," he said.

"Why do it, then?" Silas asked, almost reverently.

"Because it's already happening," Henry said. "This gives it a compass and a map."

Helen looked at Silas.

"And because silence hasn't kept us safe," she added.

Silas let out a slow breath.

"If I take this case," he said, "I'll be watched."

"You're right," Henry said.

"But I'll still be able to go home," Silas acknowledged.

Henry didn't deny it.

Silas felt something like shame, but he didn't allow himself the comfort of naming it as virtue.

"You understand," Silas said, "that I can't stop what isn't written in the official record or what is written by the press."

"I'm not asking you to."

"What are you asking, then?"

Henry leaned forward.

"That you make it harder for them to say they didn't know," he said.

Silas looked down at the table.

"And if they punish you anyway?" he asked.

Henry's voice was steady.

"Then I guess it will be clear why the case mattered."

Helen spoke again.

"We've already talked about what changes," she said. "Routes. Who answers the door. That kind of thing."

Silas looked up sharply.

"You've planned for this?"

"We plan for most things."

Silas picked up his jacket at last. He didn't go home. He returned to his office after dark and turned on only the desk lamp. The light was contained and deliberate, the way he had always preferred it.

He opened Henry's file and saw what had always been there — lawful actions, clean procedure, a sequence that closed itself without friction.

For the first time, the order didn't reassure him.

SIX
A Name Cannot Think for You

And then came Mary Ellen Wagner.

They met in church, though they remembered nothing of the sermon that day. What Silas remembered was that she didn't avert her eyes when suffering was mentioned. She treated truth like a fact rather than a threat.

She worked in the agricultural office, copied numbers neatly onto carbon forms, and walked home the same route each evening. That routine was a show of her dignity. Silas noticed her because she didn't waste words and because the silence around her felt meditative.

They became engaged quietly. There were no announcements outside of family and a few close friends. A ring and a future with a wide-open invitation were all they needed.

She died six months before the wedding. The combination of rain, a curve in the road, and a swerve in the wrong direction. And as quickly as the invitation came, it was rescinded, and no one asked his permission.

People told him it was God's will. He accepted the phrase because it allowed the conversation to end. What he didn't accept was the implication that suffering required no response.

That night, he sat in his kitchen with a Cardinals game humming through static. He wasn't listening for runs or innings. He listened for endurance, a game that went on while his world didn't. The announcer's voice, faint and distant, made him understand something philosophy never had: time does not honor grief.

After Mary Ellen, his silence changed. It was no longer reflective. It became defensive.

Caution worked, or pretended. The distinction blurred over time.

In Greenville, restraint was not merely encouraged; it was praised as maturity.

It was two years later, – long before Henry Logan, long before the federal courtrooms that would force him to choose sides, – that Silas faced his first decision that mattered.

He was a young attorney then. His office was above a shuttered insurance agency.

A Negro widow named Mrs. Craw came to him, wearing gloves in June and holding papers with shaking hands. Her husband had died. The bank intended to claim her home. Land, technically, she could not prove she had rights to because her husband had never titled it correctly.

The law was clear: the house could be taken.

The town was clearer: let it be taken.

The Thorn name hovered in the room even before he spoke. It suggested the expected outcome without argument. A Thorn didn't complicate matters already resolved. He was there to smooth, not to stop.

Silas felt the weight of lineage as pride and as instruction.

"These matters," his father would have said, "resolve themselves when left alone."

But Mary Ellen was also in that room, though she had been dead two years, and his only photograph of her was stowed away in his briefcase. Her absence had become a voice – not instructive, but reminding:

You can lose everything anyway. Choose what you won't regret.

He sat in silence long enough that Mrs. Craw stopped speaking. She began to apologize, thinking she had asked too much.

Silas finally inhaled.

"The law is against you," he said.

Her eyes fell.

"But that does not mean I will be."

The words surprised even him. Once spoken, they could not be taken back.

What unnerved him later was not that the victory was partial, but that even partial resistance had marked him.

He won her a delay. Not victory, time.

She lived in that house until winter, then she died.

People whispered afterward that Silas Thorn III had changed.

That, in a town that feared questions, was questionable, at best.

Silas understood then that the Thorn name would protect him only so long as he used it predictably.

He didn't retreat from that knowledge. He compartmentalized it.

Now, he's thirty-eight, unmarried, and still has no children. The Silas name will likely end with him.

He didn't mourn that. He has never believed legacy should outlive integrity.

A Thorn, the town believes, is supposed to be a pillar. This one is instead a mirror. People see in him not who he is, but who they fear being after they've been exposed.

And interruptions, in Mississippi, can be treated harshly.

That night, after helping Mrs. Craw, after the town murmured its disapproval, Silas sat again in his dark kitchen, radio tuned high enough to hear a Cardinals game cracking through southern air in atmospheric waves.

He waited again for endurance because some things are worth holding onto even when nothing answers back.

Silas Thomas Thorn III is not the continuation of a lineage. He is its interruption.

PART III: ESCALATION

SEVEN
The Letter from Jackson

The letter was not long. It didn't accuse or even advise him not to do what he had already resolved to do. It was written in the language of professionalism and constraint, careful enough to sound courteous.

It addressed, hypothetically, the viability of certain federal civil rights filings originating in Mississippi. It acknowledged jurisdiction. It noted precedent. It conceded that federal review existed precisely for circumstances in which State remedies proved inadequate.

The statement noted that such filings were considered "strategically isolating, institutionally disruptive, and unlikely to yield durable relief."

He folded the letter, smoothing the crease with his thumb.

It had arrived two days before he intended to file Henry's suit. That timing mattered.

He didn't sit down or drink the coffee. He ate the leftover cornbread Helen had pressed into his hands the night before, still wrapped in tin foil, crumbs scattering onto the counter. It was dense and faintly sweet. It was the kind of food that preceded physical labor.

His house was quiet, the windows were open, and a breeze gently tickled the curtains. The locusts had not yet begun in earnest.

Silas placed the new letter into his briefcase, in the private slot, along with his deceased fiancée's picture.

He told himself this was for reference. He didn't tell himself the truth – that once he spoke the letter aloud, it would cease to belong to him alone.

At the office, the day seemed to unfold sideways.

Mrs. Bladen brought him more coffee before being asked. She had learned, over time, which questions were not requests for information but bids for reassurance.

This time, he didn't reassure her.

By midday, he had reread the letter with a pen in hand. The margins remained clean. There was nothing to underline that would not later appear damning.

The letter was unsigned. That, too, was deliberate.

He recognized the cadence, not a voice, exactly, but a shared rhythm common to men who had clerked together, who had learned to speak in ways that sounded detached while accomplishing alignment. Men who would later say, truthfully, that they had never told him not to file. Only that he should consider what filing would cost.

Silas understood that this case would fail the moment it appeared to be about Henry Logan alone. One man could be dismissed as unlucky, inattentive, or exceptional in the wrong direction. The law had learned how to absorb singular harm without consequence. What it could not so easily dismiss was provable repetition.

The theory, then, was not that Henry had been treated unlawfully in isolation, but that the State had constructed a system in which legality functioned as a filter rather than a safeguard, impartial in language, selective in application.

Under color of law, local officials enforced ordinances that were facially indifferent and operationally precise, producing outcomes so consistent they could not be explained as discretion. Equal protection was denied not by statute, but by pattern. Due process was hollowed not by performance, but by predictability. The injury was cumulative, ordinary, and therefore invisible to anyone who insisted on viewing each act as an isolated event.

His carefully prepared brief had been read and re-read multiple times. As he went through with it, he anxiously weighed the option of withdrawing, aware that such a decision would cost him a budding friendship with Henry.

"You can lose everything anyway. Choose what you won't regret."

That afternoon, Silas drove to the district courthouse in Jackson. He realized there was no turning back now.

COMPLAINT

**In the United States District Court
For The Southern District of Mississippi
Jackson Division**

HENRY LOGAN

    Plaintiff,

Nuremberg, Mississippi

v.

CV-1965-______________

STATE OF MISSISSIPPI

Defendant.

COMPLAINT FOR DECLARATORY AND INJUNCTIVE RELIEF

COMES NOW the Plaintiff, Henry Logan, by and through counsel, and brings this action against the State of Mississippi, and alleges as follows:

I. JURISDICTION AND VENUE

1.   This action arises under the Constitution and laws of the United States, including the Fourteenth Amendment and federal civil rights statutes enacted pursuant thereto.

2.   Jurisdiction is proper under 28 U.S.C. § 1343 and related provisions conferring jurisdiction upon federal courts to redress the deprivation of constitutional rights under color of state law.

3.   Venue is proper in this district because the acts complained of occurred within this district and the Plaintiff resides herein.

II. PARTIES

4.   Plaintiff Henry Logan is a citizen of the United States and a resident of Myrtle County, Mississippi.

5.   Defendant State of Mississippi is responsible for the enforcement, administration, and supervision of local ordinances and policies challenged herein.

III. FACTUAL ALLEGATIONS

6.   Plaintiff is a Negro citizen who, at all relevant times, complied with the written laws and ordinances of Myrtle County to the extent reasonably possible.

7.   Defendant, through local officials acting under color of law, enforced facially neutral ordinances governing curfew, loitering, and public order in a manner that systematically burdened Negro residents while permitting similarly situated White residents to remain unimpeded.

8.   Enforcement decisions were made pursuant to unjust and discriminatory custom, practice, and administrative discretion rather than individualized assessment.

9.   Plaintiff was arrested, charged, convicted, and incarcerated under such facially neutral ordinances despite the absence of any conduct posing a threat to public safety.

10.   These actions were not isolated, accidental, or aberrational, but consistent with an enduring pattern of selective enforcement.

IV. CLAIMS FOR RELIEF

COUNT I – VIOLATION OF EQUAL PROTECTION (Fourteenth Amendment)

11.   Plaintiff incorporates herein the allegations heretofore stated in paragraphs 1-10 as if set forth herein in full.
12.   Defendant's enforcement practices denied Plaintiff equal protection of the laws by selectively applying ordinances based on race.
13.   Such enforcement cannot be justified by legitimate governmental interest and operates as a racial classification in effect.

COUNT II – VIOLATION OF DUE PROCESS (Fourteenth Amendment)

14.	Plaintiff incorporates herein the allegations heretofore stated in paragraphs 1-13 as if set forth herein in full.
15.	Plaintiff was deprived of liberty without meaningful notice or fair application of the law.
16.	Ordinances enforced against Plaintiff vested unbridled discretion in enforcement officials, rendering compliance uncertain and punishment arbitrary and capricious.

V. RELIEF REQUESTED

Plaintiff respectfully requests that this Court:

Declare Defendant's enforcement practices unconstitutional;
Enjoin Defendant from continuing such practices;
Grant such further relief as justice requires.

Respectfully submitted,
Silas T. Thorn III
Attorney for Plaintiff

SEVEN AND ONE-HALF
Mississippi or Germany

Silas detoured near the Capitol building and walked, the heat rising in waves from the pavement. He passed men in rolled-up sleeves, and women carrying paper bags folded neatly at the top. Everyone appeared busy without appearing rushed. The undefeated rhythm of city life went unimpeded.

His colleague, Harold Greene, received him into his expansive office. Greene listened without interruption as Silas laid the original, unsigned letter on the desk between them.

Greene didn't touch it. Instead, he leaned sideways onto his armrest and said, "You know what this is?"

"Yes," Silas replied.

"You also know what it isn't?"

"Yes."

"It's permission to abandon you."

Silas chose to remain silent.

"They didn't send this to stop you," Greene continued. "They sent it so they wouldn't have to follow you. They'll say you were warned, and they won't be wrong."

They spoke briefly about the documents, the timing, and the difference between winning a case and surviving it. Greene didn't argue with Silas. He spoke plainly and left details unsaid.

When Silas stood to leave, Greene hesitated.

"There are people who will stop returning your calls," he said. "Not dramatically. Not all at once. Just…eventually."

"I've noticed," Silas said.

"Some of them will tell themselves it's temporary."

"And the others?"

"They'll decide your presence is a professional or personal embarrassment."

Silas left and walked two blocks to a café he had visited with his father when he was younger. He ordered the Tuesday special – meatloaf and mashed potatoes. The plate arrived steaming, and the waitress topped off his sweet tea. He ate alone.

At a nearby table, two young court clerks argued about baseball with the seriousness of men who had not yet learned how fragile distraction could be.

When the waitress refilled his water, she said, "You look like you're carrying something heavy."

He smiled. "Yeah, I'm a lawyer."

She laughed. "Well, that explains it."

Back in Greenville, the shift didn't arrive as a parade. It revealed itself gradually, like a change in the barometric pressure before a summer storm.

A judge who once lingered after hearings now kept his eyes on the docket. A colleague who had borrowed books from Silas's shelves stopped doing so. Invitations thinned, conversations shortened, yet no one said anything explicit.

One evening, Silas stopped at the grocery store on his way home. He bought bread, eggs, a small cut of pork, and a bag of apples. At the checkout, he realized he had picked up two identical loaves of bread.

The boy sacking the groceries – no more than sixteen – grinned. "Do you eat a lot of sandwiches?"

Silas looked at the bread, then laughed loudly. "No," he said. "Distracted, I guess."

At home, he cooked simply. Fried pork, apples sliced thin with a little sugar, and eggs scrambled soft. He ate standing at the counter, jacket still on, tie loosened but not removed.

Later, he opened the briefcase again and took out the Jackson letters.

Then he set them aside and removed the complaint he had drafted for Henry.

He read it a couple of times but made no changes.

Before turning in, Silas reached for a book he had not opened since law school. He didn't read long. What unnerved him was not the scale of the crimes described there, but the familiarity of the defenses – expectations, obedience, and permanence. Men insisting they had acted within a system they didn't design but dutifully maintained.

He closed the book and returned it to the shelf, irritated with himself for having reached for it at all.

Mississippi was not Germany, he scolded himself.

Silas read the complaint one final time. He still didn't make any changes.

The next morning, he drove to Jackson.

Nuremberg, Mississippi

EIGHT
The Filing

Henry's workday began earlier now. Arriving early extended the margin he could still control. He unlocked the gates and reviewed orders that had already been reviewed. Preparation substituted for certainty.

Invoices that once cleared within days lingered. A supplier asked whether the account would remain "active." The word carried no accusation, only contingency. Henry answered carefully.

Nothing was denied outright. Everything was delayed long enough to require an explanation.

By mid-morning, he had learned to recognize which calls would be returned and which would not. He adjusted his routes accordingly, choosing streets that kept him visible without inviting comment.

He stopped mentioning the case unless asked. When asked, he spoke narrowly – dates, filings, schedules. He didn't editorialize.

Compliance didn't restore what had been lost. It only prevented further loss. Henry understood the distinction.

He had done everything the court required, and nothing more.

That evening, Silas called to review the draft.

The call was efficient. Pages were discussed. Language refined. A concession tightened. Silas's voice carried the tone of progress.

"We're in a good position," Silas said. "They're listening."

Henry said nothing for a moment.

He considered explaining what had changed. He wondered how much of it would be documented.

"They are," Henry said finally.

Silas took the answer as agreement.

"We should avoid escalating," Silas continued. "Let the record develop. The calmer we remain, the harder it is for them to dismiss us."

Henry listened. He had learned the discipline of listening long before it had been praised.

Silas's caution cost him nothing he could not recover. Henry's cost accrued daily.

The week ended without further incident.

No citations. No warnings. No disruptions.

That absence should have reassured Henry. Instead, it required another layer of vigilance.

When Silas mentioned, almost in passing, that a bench trial might be cleaner given the circumstances, Henry just listened.

Cleaner, Henry thought, meant quieter. It meant fewer eyes.

"Are you sure?" Henry said.

He had started to trust Silas. He had never stopped distrusting others.

By Friday, Henry's supervisor suggested a temporary reduction in hours. It was framed as flexibility.

Henry thanked him anyway, though he felt anything but thankful in that moment.

That night, Helen recalculated again.

Nothing had been taken formally.

Everything had narrowed.

***

The clerk stamped the filing without looking up. If a sound were ever administrative, this was it. The paper slid across the counter as though nothing had happened, as though the act itself had been incidental rather than irreversible.

Silas waited – briefly, foolishly – expecting more. A pause. A question. Anything. The clerk reached for the next document. The line shifted.

That was it.

The complaint – Logan v. Mississippi – was now part of the record.

Silas stepped outside into the heat with the peculiar sensation of having misplaced something important. Not lost, exactly, but without the routine inevitability that usually followed his filings.

Driving back to Greenville, he understood what had disturbed him. The filing itself had never been the risk. The law absorbed documents easily. It was what followed – what moved without paper, without transcript, without appeal – that mattered.

By the time he reached town, the sun was high enough to wash out the color from the courthouse steps.

The first sign came that afternoon.

Henry didn't call. That alone was not unusual. Henry was careful about phones. He preferred conversation when he could survey the room around him.

The call came instead from a foreman, Silas recognized by voice but not by name – a man who had once waved Henry over in the square as if waving at a friend.

"Mr. Thorn," the man said, clearing his throat. "Thought you should know."

Silas listened.

The job Henry had been promised – three weeks of steady work repairing storage sheds along the rail spur ... has been "put on hold." No timeline. No explanation. Budget concerns, perhaps. Or scheduling.

"We'll circle back," the man said, using a familiar but unreliable phrase.

Silas thanked him and hung up.

He didn't write anything down.

By evening, Helen knew.

Henry came home earlier than usual. He washed his hands at the sink longer than necessary, which had become routine lately and was a sign of internal conflict. It was like the running water at home allowed his thoughts to flow freer.

"Did something happen?" she asked, keeping her voice even.

Henry dried his hands. "They don't need me tomorrow."

"Tomorrow," she repeated.

She didn't ask why.

Helen had prepared their meal of beans and rice with calculated intention, stretching what remained in the pantry as far as she could, never once complaining. The children talked about school. Henry listened. He smiled at the appropriate places. He didn't mention the job.

They were growing children and ate as a mandate. Helen gave them some cornbread and buttermilk, which is comforting and familiar in this part of the country.

Later, when the children were asleep, Helen said, "This is it, isn't it?"

"Yes," he said.

She sat at the table. "That was fast."

Henry leaned back slightly. "I expected faster."

She looked at him. "Already?"

"They would have looked strange if they waited," he said. "This way it still looks like a coincidence."

"How do we adjust?"

Henry exhaled. "We always find a way."

They talked quietly – about groceries, about routes, about whether Helen should delay the trip she had planned to her sister's. Nothing dramatic. Nothing that would sound urgent if overheard.

But when Henry lay awake that night, staring at the ceiling, he understood something he had not articulated before – the punishment was not the loss of wages alone. It was the recalibration of expectation. The narrowing of the future until it became manageable by others.

Across town, Silas sat at his desk and reread the complaint.

He had already received two messages that day from colleagues who said nothing substantive. "Checking in on you." "Heard you were busy." Each note carefully avoided the case itself, as though the subject were contagious.

The phone rang after 9 p.m.

Judge Whitaker's voice was cordial and familiar.

"I wanted to give you a bit of friendly advice," Whitaker said.

Silas listened.

"This kind of thing," the judge continued, "has a way of...expanding. People feel accused even when they're not named."

Silas said nothing.

"You've built a respectable practice," Whitaker went on. "It would be a shame to jeopardize it over a matter that – if we're being honest – won't resolve the way you think it will."

Silas understood the offer embedded in the warning.

"I appreciate your concern," he said.

There was a pause.

"Of course," Whitaker replied. "I knew you would."

The line went dead.

Silas didn't move for several minutes.

He thought of Henry standing at his sink. He thought of Helen counting food. He thought of the Jackson letter, still folded in his briefcase.

The law had not moved against him yet, but it had turned.

That night, Silas dreamed he was standing in a courtroom without walls. The bench was empty. The rules were posted, neatly typed, but no one enforced them. When he spoke, his voice carried, but no one wrote it down.

He woke before dawn, his heart steady, and his understanding intact.

At the start of his workday, the second consequence arrived.

Mrs. Bladen met him at the door of the office, purse still over her shoulder.

"I should have told you yesterday," she said. "The bank called. They're revisiting the line of credit."

"Revisiting?"

"They said it was routine."

He thanked her.

"I've worked for you a long time," she said carefully. "I don't need to know details. But I need to know whether I should worry."

"You shouldn't," he said.

She searched his face, then nodded, not reassured, but loyal.

When she left, Silas sat alone and understood that the case had already escaped the courtroom.

And it had predictably chosen Henry first.

***

By Thursday, coincidence had become a pattern.

Henry stood on the square after sunrise, toolbox in hand, and his posture dispassionate. As usual, he didn't linger. He occupied the space the way one does when occupying space has always required negotiation.

Two men he recognized passed without acknowledging him. Another looked at him, then looked away. A truck slowed, then continued through the intersection without stopping.

Henry waited the length of time that could still be described as reasonable. Then he left.

At home, Helen reorganized the pantry. The shelves were rearranged so that what would spoil soonest sat in front. Flour was transferred into smaller containers. Sugar was rationed. The jar of coffee grounds – already scarce – was set toward the back.

When Henry came in, she said only, "I'm going to make soup tonight."

"That's fine," he shrugged.

The children didn't notice anything unusual. That, Helen thought, was both a mercy and a warning.

Across town, Silas received his first refusal.

It came from a man he had known for years, an attorney who shared his taste for long lunches and quiet argument, and who had once confided doubts about the very ordinances now under challenge.

"I can't co-sign that brief," the man said. "It wouldn't be in anyone's best interest."

Silas asked, "Because it's wrong?"

"No," the man said quickly. "Because it's radioactive. I admire what you're doing," the man continued. "But I have a family. I have a position. I have obligations that aren't concerned with principled stands."

Silas let the sentence rest.

"I understand."

And he did.

The second refusal was shorter.

"I can't be associated with this," the voice said. "It won't help anyone if I lose what little influence I have."

The third didn't return his call at all.

By Friday, the absence had shape.

That evening, Silas attended a church supper he had attended for years. Fried catfish, green beans, and pound cake cut into identical squares. The conversations were polite in that Southern restrained way. Several people asked about his health. One talked about the weather.

No one mentioned the case.

When he sat down at his usual table, the seat beside him remained empty. Eventually, a woman he didn't know well sat there, offering a quick smile.

Silas ate slowly, eventually getting up to leave.

On his way out, the pastor grabbed his shoulder.

"You've always been thoughtful," the Reverend said. "I hope you'll continue to be."

Silas knew a warning when he heard one.

That same night, a deputy stopped Helen on her way back from her sister's.

It was not aggressive, nor was it violent.

Her taillight, the deputy said, was flickering. He asked where she was headed. He asked where she had been. He asked whether the children were tired.

Helen answered carefully.

The stop lasted long enough to deliver its message.

When she told Henry about it, she didn't raise her voice. She explained it like she was talking about a shift in the wind.

"They wanted to be seen," she said. "Not to do anything. To let me know they were watching."

"That's enough," Henry said.

Later, when Helen lay awake, she thought of Silas's face at the kitchen table – the way his confidence had faltered not from fear, but from recognition. He had believed, until recently, that exposure was accidental. He was learning otherwise.

Saturday morning, Silas received a letter – this time from his bank.

The language was courteous. The concern was procedural. A review of his accounts. A reassessment of risk. No obvious urgency or determination.

He read it, then placed it beside the Jackson letters in his briefcase.

The symmetry didn't escape him.

That afternoon, Silas drove past the Logan house without stopping. He told himself it was because he didn't want to intrude. Or because he didn't want to become another variable they had to plan around. Or because nothing he could say would improve the situation.

Those explanations were all partially true.

The truth he didn't articulate was simpler. He didn't yet know how to look Henry in the eye and admit that the consequences had arrived sooner than he had expected.

Instead, he went home and cooked for himself. He over-salted the meat. He didn't notice until it was too late.

Sunday morning, Silas received the call that clarified everything.

It came from Robert Bullock, a senior attorney in Jackson – someone who had once encouraged Silas's ambitions, who had written him a letter of recommendation that now sat framed in his office.

"I wanted to be direct," Bullock said. "There are people who believe this case crosses a line."

Silas listened anxiously.

"They believe you're accusing the state itself," he continued. "Not officials. Not policies. The STATE."

"And is that belief incorrect?" Silas asked.

There was a pause.

"It's destabilizing," Bullock said finally.

Silas understood then that this was the defection he had been waiting for – not the quiet withdrawal of convenience, but the unmistakable arrival of chosen sides.

"I won't be able to support you in any capacity," he said.

Silas closed his eyes briefly. "Thank you for telling me."

When the call ended, Silas sat alone and experienced something unfamiliar – not fear or anger, but a reckoning. The field of possible outcomes had collapsed. What remained was not strategy, but stamina.

That evening, Silas finally went to see Henry.

When Helen opened the door, she didn't smile. She simply stepped aside.

Henry was at the table, the Negro Motorist Green Book still where it had been days before. The book had not moved. That, Silas realized, was its own kind of statement.

"I should have come sooner," Silas said.

"You came when you could."

Henry offered Silas a seat, which he graciously accepted.

Silas told him about the bank, the recent refusals, and the ominous call from Jackson.

Henry listened intently.

When Silas finished, Henry said, "They're doing what they do best."

"And you?" Silas asked.

"We're adjusting."

Silas took a deep breath. "I underestimated how quickly it would start. I thought there would be…lag," Silas said. "That there would be more deniability."

Helen spoke from the counter. "There's always deniability," she said. "That's how it works."

"I should have prepared you better," Silas replied. "I must admit that I have a newfound respect for both of you. You have more courage than anyone I know."

Henry, realizing the dilemma that Silas faced, passed along his heartiest wisdom: "Courage isn't beginning an impossible task. People start every new year doing that. Courage is finishing that task no matter the obstacles."

That night, driving home, Silas understood the distinction he had missed. The law does not escalate gradually. It waits until it is certain, then it moves efficiently.

And it does not begin with the man who files.

It begins with the man who must live with the outcome, even before the judge makes a ruling.

***

Silas realized that punishment wasn't dependent on anger. Instead, it simply needed everyone to agree.

By Monday morning, the town had settled into a new alignment. Nothing had changed officially. No statements were issued. The ordinances remained where they had always been, phrased in language that suggested what was expected.

But the margins had suddenly narrowed, much the way the afternoon shadows always had for Henry.

Henry woke early and got dressed, as if work still waited somewhere that punctuality might summon it back. He shaved, then put on a clean shirt. He packed his lunch anyway – two sandwiches Helen had wrapped tightly to preserve their moisture and his dignity.

When he stepped onto the porch, the neighborhood was already awake. A truck idled across the way. A man Henry didn't recognize leaned against it, not watching him directly, but not watching either.

Henry walked past without speaking.

He took the longer route to the square.

He didn't find work.

By mid-morning, he had been stopped twice – once by a patrol car that slowed enough to read his posture, once by a deputy who asked whether everything was all right.

"Yes, sir," Henry said both times.

Everything was all right.

At home, Helen waited.

She had baked bread that morning, stretching the flour with care, adding water slowly until the dough cooperated. She cleaned as she went, not from compulsion but from anxiety. The radio stayed off because she needed to hear herself think.

When Henry returned earlier than the children expected, they looked up from the table.

"Daddy?" the youngest asked.

"I'm home," Henry said. It was true.

That afternoon, the phone rang. Silas answered on the second ring.

The voice on the line belonged to Judge Whitaker again, but this time the tone had shifted. The courtesy remained, but the warmth had been withdrawn.

"I wanted to let you know," Whitaker said, "that I've been asked to recuse myself from any matters involving your client."

Silas absorbed this.

"Asked," he repeated.

"Yes," Whitaker said. "It was suggested that my familiarity with you might create an appearance of bias."

"And do you believe it does?" Silas asked.

There was a pause. "Belief isn't the issue," Whitaker said. "Perception is."

Silas thanked him and hung up.

Within the hour, a second call arrived – this one from a clerk who had once been eager to please, now efficient to the point of being cold.

"There's been a reassignment," the clerk said. "Your motions will be routed differently going forward."

Silas asked nothing further.

By evening, the message was clear enough to be read without translation – the system was not attacking him. It was repositioning itself around him.

That night, Helen did something she had not done in years. She packed a bag. Not everything. Not even enough to suggest flight, but enough to suggest readiness.

Henry noticed.

"For the children?" he asked.

"For me," she said. "In case I need to leave quickly."

"Where would you go?"

She stopped for a moment. "A place where I don't have to justify who I am," she said.

They ate in silence. The children sensed something had changed, but lacked the language to name it. Afterward, Henry walked them through their lessons, voice steady, correcting them gently.

When the house came to a rest, Helen sat at the table with the Negro Motorist Green Book open in front of her.

She traced a route with a pen, and then stopped.

Across town, Silas sat alone in his office.

The Jackson letter lay open on the desk now. The bank notice beside it. A stack of returned phone messages, most of them impersonal, none of them helpful.

He had lost something he could not replace. Not clients or credit. Illusion.

The belief that the law's failures were accidental. The confidence that objectivity could be reclaimed through better argument. The principle that his own insulation was evidence of fairness rather than inheritance.

He thought of the book he had opened nights earlier – the one he had closed too quickly. He pulled it from the shelf again.

This time, he read.

What bothered him was not the heinousness of the crimes described, but the ordinariness of the men who committed them. Their insistence that they had acted within frameworks they neither authored nor questioned. Their reliance on steadiness as defense.

He closed the book slowly.

Mississippi was not Germany, but the defenses were familiar.

The next morning, the retaliation crossed a line that could not be stepped back over.

Henry was arrested at 6:40 a.m.

The charge was loitering.

The deputy was apologetic. Henry didn't resist, nor did he argue, only hesitating to ask whether he could put on his jacket.

"You won't need it long," the deputy said.

Helen watched from the doorway. She didn't cry or speak.

She handed Henry his watch.

At the jail, Henry sat on a bench that smelled of disinfectant and desperation. The charge was processed. The time recorded. The bond was set at an amount calculated, costly enough to remind him not to forget.

He was released before noon.

When Silas arrived at the Logan house later that day, Henry was already home.

They sat at the table where the Green Book still lay.

Silas didn't apologize. He didn't explain.

He said, "This is what it looks like."

Henry replied, "Yeah, I know."

Silas's voice was steady. "They will keep doing this."

"Yes."

"And it will not stop with you."

Henry looked up. "I told you that."

Silas exhaled. "I need to ask you something. If this ends badly, if the case fails, if the court closes ranks, will you regret filing?"

After a meditative pause, Henry said, finally, "No."

"Why not?"

"Because then the record will show they had the chance to stop," Henry said. "And chose not to."

Silas felt something settle into place – certainly not comfort or resolve. It was now about position.

"I will not withdraw," he said. "I can't now."

"I didn't think you would."

Helen added, "They're counting on you to grow tired."

Silas stood. "I won't. Right or wrong, we're now joined at the hip."

He didn't say it heroically. He said it as fact.

Helen had long acquired the ability to interpret environments with the same attentiveness others apply to facial expressions – identifying areas of tension, change, or persistence. She maintained this insight discreetly, along with other observations seldom requested: knowledge of which doors became difficult in warmer temperatures, awareness of subtle vocal changes after dusk, and recognition of the conditional nature of certain acts of kindness.

Helen's appreciation for Henry was pragmatic. She valued his conviction that fear could be managed through reason, and considered it her responsibility to support him where his trust made him vulnerable.

In her current situation, she relied not on hope or frustration, but on a sense of competence – the assurance cultivated through ongoing attentiveness and an understanding that, at times, remaining passive equated to negligence.

When Silas left the house, the light was fading, and the street was quiet. Driving away, Silas understood that the law was no longer the arena.

It was the artifact.

What mattered now was not whether justice would be done, but whether it would be named before being buried under bureaucracy.

And for the first time since filing the case, Silas didn't wonder whether he had gone too far.

He wondered only how long the truth was willing to wait.

EIGHT AND THREE-FOURTHS
No Response

The complaint was filed on a Tuesday.

Silas watched the clerk stamp the document and slide it into a stack already waiting. There was no hesitation. No comment. No acknowledgment beyond the motion itself.

"That's it?" Silas asked.

"That's it," the clerk replied.

He and Henry stepped outside together. The afternoon was sunny but otherwise ordinary. Traffic moved through the intersection as it always had.

Henry said nothing.

Silas expected the quiet to feel temporary.

It didn't.

The next morning arrived without incident. No call or messages. Henry went to work. Silas went to his office. Paper moved in both directions without reference to what had been filed the day before.

At the courthouse, the routine held steady.

Files were requested. Forms were stamped. Names were called and answered. No one mentioned the complaint. No one avoided it either. It was as though the document had entered a layer of the building that didn't overlap with speech.

Henry returned to the office later that week.

The clerk greeted him the same way he always had.

"Morning," he said.

Henry nodded.

The file was retrieved. The pages were turned. The notation was still there.

"Still under review," the clerk said.

Henry waited.

"Is that because of the filing?" he asked.

The clerk blinked, then shook his head.

"No," he said. "This is separate."

"Separate how?" Henry asked.

The clerk shrugged. "Different track."

Henry nodded.

Nothing in the clerk's posture suggested deception. He was not withholding. He was reporting.

The system had not resisted the complaint.

It had absorbed it.

That night, Silas reviewed the filing at his desk, searching for something that should have triggered action. He found nothing. The document was clear, restrained, and thorough.

That, he realized, was another problem.

By the end of the week, it was clear that nothing would happen quickly.

By the end of the second, it was clear that nothing would happen at all unless it were forced.

The silence was not indifference; it was control.

The complaint had entered the record.

The record had closed around it.

NINE
A System Cross-Examined

The arguments were framed narrowly.

Silas avoided language that suggested accusation. He emphasized process, intent, and reasonableness. Each sentence was apportioned to reassure. Each concession was made early, before it could be demanded.

He told himself this was discipline.

Silas noticed how often his words returned to him unchanged. Phrases he used in filings reappeared in replies. Arguments he framed narrowly were echoed back with equal restraint. The system didn't resist him; it mirrored him.

That resemblance comforted him.

When the State spoke, it echoed him. The same language. The same assurance that nothing improper had occurred, only misunderstandings corrected through orderly means.

After one hearing, a colleague from another firm slapped Silas on the shoulder.

"You're handling this the right way," he said. "Keeping it professional."

Silas accepted the praise. He believed it was earned.

Compliments arrived framed as relief. Judges appreciated counsel who didn't escalate. Clerks moved his filings without comment. The absence of friction was treated as success.

No one asked what the restraint cost.

An internal memo circulated within the State's office.

It praised the plaintiff's restraint. It noted that counsel appeared disinclined toward theatrics. It suggested that this posture reduced risk.

The memo was brief. Its tone was calm.

Silas never saw it.

What he sensed instead was alignment. The system appeared responsive, attentive, even cooperative. That responsiveness felt earned.

Silas mistook accommodation for progress.

Henry began to notice changes that were not announced.

Clients delayed returning calls. A supervisor asked whether his involvement in the case might be "temporary." A bank officer suggested that discretion was advisable.

No one threatened him. Each interaction arrived politely, framed as concern.

Henry didn't name these encounters as retaliation. Naming required proof, and proof required records. What he experienced left none.

Instead, he adjusted. He spoke less. He chose his words carefully. He began to anticipate which topics shortened conversations and avoided them.

This, too, felt normal.

What Silas experienced as professional affirmation, Henry experienced as contraction. The system didn't need to choose between them. It could reward caution in one place and enforce silence in another.

Silas didn't request a bench trial yet.

He told himself there was still room to persuade. That escalation would be premature. That timing mattered.

He believed he was protecting Henry by moving slowly.

What he didn't yet see was the distance opening between intent and effect. His careful pacing was already producing consequences he could not feel.

The file grew thicker. Dates accumulated. Nothing dramatic occurred.

That, Silas believed, was where he wanted to be.

Nuremberg, Mississippi

TEN
Jury Duty

The courtroom never identifies itself as hostile because, to most of the townspeople, it isn't.

The benches were already filled when Henry entered, though the room was far from crowded. Most of the faces belonged to men who had taken the morning off from work because it was expected of them, or because it allowed them to be seen taking it. A few women sat together near the aisle, coats folded over their arms, hands clasped in a manner that suggested waiting rather than watching.

Judge Mathewson's entrance was surprisingly casual. There was no gavel strike – only the clerk's voice, measured and precise, instructing the room to rise. Mathewson nodded, already reading, already elsewhere.

The clerk began calling names.

Each response was recorded methodically, though nothing appeared to hinge on them. Occupations were noted. Addresses confirmed. A few men were asked whether they knew the plaintiff. One smiled faintly and said he didn't, though his eyes didn't leave Henry.

Silas rose when permitted. He asked about impartiality. About fairness. About the ability to weigh evidence without prejudice.

The answers came easily.

"Yes, sir."

"I believe I could."

"I don't see color."

Henry watched as each answer was accepted at face value, as though the words themselves satisfied the requirement.

When the State began its questions, the tone shifted – not in volume, but in direction. The questions narrowed. Emphasis moved from principle to comfort.

Would serving on the jury be a hardship?

Did anyone feel uneasy sitting in judgment of a local ordinance?

Was anyone concerned that neighbors might misunderstand a verdict?

Hands rose then. A few men excused themselves with visible relief. The clerk recorded each reason with the same impersonal interest.

By mid-morning, Henry understood something he had not known to articulate before – the jury was not being assembled. It was being shaped.

The clerk approached Silas during a recess, her voice low.

"They'll finish selection today," she said. It was not advice. It was information.

Silas had already reached the same conclusion. He also knew what that meant.

He requested a sidebar when proceedings resumed. Judge Mathewson listened without interruption as Silas raised concerns about representativeness, about exclusion patterns too consistent to ignore.

Mathewson adjusted his glasses.

"Counsel," he said unemotionally, "this court is satisfied that all statutory requirements have been met."

There was no rebuke in the tone. There was also no opening.

Silas returned to his seat. Henry didn't look at him. He was studying the jury box, already occupied, already decided.

When the final panel was sworn, Henry counted. Twelve men. All White. All local. All were confident in their presence.

He felt no anger. What he felt was recognition. This, he understood, was how it was done.

Silas still didn't request a bench trial.

He told himself it was a strategy. That juries, even homogeneous ones, could surprise. That procedure allowed for persuasion.

He didn't say – would not say – that asking too soon would look like retreat.

That night, in his office, Silas reviewed his notes and reassured himself with doctrine. Precedent allowed discretion. Judges were constrained. Harm could be mitigated by careful argument.

Reducing harm, he reasoned, was not the same as surrendering.

He didn't yet ask what it meant if harm was the system's preferred output.

Silas drove to the Logans' house but parked and remained in the car.

The engine cooled. The ticking beneath the hood slowed, then stopped. The porch behind him remained unlit. He understood that it was not an oversight. Helen and Henry knew when light served them and when it didn't.

He placed the key back into the ignition only after the house had fully disappeared into darkness.

The drive home felt sedated, as though the road itself had begun imposing its own guardrails. He took note of intersections he had passed through for years without memory — where sight lines narrowed, where buildings sat closer to the street, where patrol cars pounced. These were not new features. They had rarely required his attention before.

That, too, unsettled him.

Silas recognized the sensation immediately and immediately dismissed it. Discomfort, he told himself, was a sign of adjustment, not danger. Awareness didn't require action. It required calibration.

At a service station near the county line, he slowed, scanning its lot. The pumps were on. There were no customers. A single attendant sat behind the glass, reading. Silas realized he had never wondered who was permitted to linger there after dark and who was not. The question arrived fully formed, as though it had been waiting for him. He didn't stop.

When he reached home, he entered quietly, as if afraid to awaken someone who was never there. He set his jacket down rather than hanging it, then corrected himself. He hung it properly and smoothed the sleeve. He washed his hands. The house was unchanged, but he was acutely aware that this was not evidence of safety, merely of stability.

He slept lightly and woke earlier than usual.

Morning returned the world to him in manageable proportions. He drank his normal coffee and read his hometown newspaper. The unease from the night before receded, even if his routine only postponed his doubt.

By habit, he reached for the paper first but found himself scanning the margins rather than the headlines. What interested him was not what had occurred, but what had been omitted. No mention of the ordinance revisions passed the previous month quietly. No acknowledgment of the clerk's sudden firing in Jackson.

He knew these details because he had begun paying attention to them. They used to be curiosities. Now they were signals.

At his desk that morning, Silas opened a fresh legal pad. He didn't title it. Instead, he began listing impressions – meetings postponed without explanation, phone calls returned hours later than usual, conversations that ended politely but abruptly. None of it would justify a complaint. All of it would, collectively, invite scrutiny.

He wrote the word *capital*, then crossed it out. He replaced it with *administration*.

Later that morning, a memorandum circulated quietly through the courthouse offices. It didn't mention names. It praised professionalism, restraint, and the importance of maintaining public confidence during periods of heightened attention.

Silas read it thoroughly. Nothing in it alarmed him. That was its design.

ELEVEN
The Courtroom Encounter

Judge Mathewson appeared like he had been seated for hours. The clerk moved with the same steady indifference he had displayed during Hosea Jones's sentencing, Henry Logan's sentence reduction, and the jury's formation and swearing-in.

When instructed, Silas rose. He didn't preface his statement. He didn't seek the room's attention.

He began as he always did when he wanted power to hear him without feeling confronted.

"Your Honor," he stated, "this motion concerns the discovery and admissibility of municipal enforcement records."

Paul Jenkins, the State's attorney, rose with authoritative precision. His posture suggested a man who had figured out how to occupy space without claiming it. He kept a small photograph in his breast pocket – his daughter at her college graduation. When he thought no one was watching, he touched it once before standing to argue.

Mathewson remained impassive. "Proceed."

Silas focused on the bench, ignoring everything else.

"The ordinance in question is facially neutral," Silas stated, conceding the premise. "This court has established that facial neutrality does not equate to fairness. However, it is often the initial question. The initial question is what the State aims to protect here."

Jenkins' mouth tightened.

Silas continued.

"Enforcement patterns are crucial when an ordinance's application relies on discretion. Here, discretion is the driving force. While the ordinance does not specify race, it functions through human choice. And human choice can be quantified."

He placed a stack of papers on the lectern.

"These are the municipal enforcement logs from the past twelve months," he explained. "They include time, location, charge, and disposition."

Jenkins raised his hand slightly. "Objection. Relevance."

Silas didn't turn or react. He remained focused on Mathewson.

"It is relevant," Silas responded calmly, "because the State plans to argue that this is standard public safety enforcement. If that is the case, the record will reflect ordinariness. If not, the record will reveal something different."

Mathewson narrowed his eyes slightly in contemplation – an expression he reserved for arguments that allowed him to seem reasonable without losing authority.

Jenkins spoke again, more cautiously now. "Your Honor, these logs – if they exist – are administrative. They do not provide evidence of discriminatory intent. They will mislead the jury, incite interpretation, and invite this case to become something it is not."

Silas kept a stone face.

"What it is not," Silas replied, "is a matter of motive. We will not be discussing what a deputy felt. We will be discussing what the ordinance does. The law does not require the court to examine a man's heart to understand his actions."

A slight rustle in the gallery indicated discomfort with statements suggesting the court could measure its own actions.

Mathewson leaned back and removed his reading glasses.

For a moment, Silas feared he had misjudged — not the argument, which was sound, but the room.

The judge was a man who disliked being asked to acknowledge patterns, as they implied design, which suggested accountability.

Mathewson's fingers brushed the file, then withdrew, as if it were scalding.

"This court is not convened to perform sociological analysis," he declared, his voice calm enough to be perceived as compassionate. "We are here to interpret an ordinance and evaluate whether it has been applied correctly in a specific instance."

Silas recognized that the judge had provided him with precisely what he needed.

"Yes, Your Honor," Silas replied. "And 'correctly' holds significance only if it can be distinguished from 'predictably.' If enforcement is consistent, the record will demonstrate that, and the jury will be reassured. If enforcement is selective, the record will reveal that, and the jury will not be misled by false neutrality."

Jenkins' tone sharpened slightly. "Counsel is attempting to try the entire town."

Silas's voice remained unchanged.

"No," he said. "I am attempting to try the ordinance. The town just happens to be where it has been enacted."

Mathewson now looked directly at him.

Silas held firm. He understood the risk: he was compelling the court to choose between appearing principled and preserving the town's comfort. Judges typically dislike being forced to choose.

An uncomfortable silence lingered.

Then Mathewson spoke.

"Motion granted in part," he announced. "Enforcement logs for the past six months will be produced. Counsel will confer to determine the format. The court will assess admissibility later."

There was no gavel.

The clerk recorded the decision with the same meticulous hand that noted everything else.

Granted in part.

It was the kind of ruling that allowed everyone to exit the room believing they had not lost.

Silas sat.

He didn't look at Henry. He waited until he sensed the room calm, then glanced to his left.

Henry's expression remained unchanged. He was focused on the judge, not Silas.

Silas experienced a brief, unfamiliar sensation – something akin to satisfaction, but not the usual professional kind. This was not a victory that shielded his client from immediate consequences.

This was a victory that compelled the system to reveal itself.

It was an uncomfortable kind of victory.

Outside the courtroom, in the hallway, Jenkins passed Silas with a polite nod.

"Creative," Jenkins remarked, a mix of compliment and insult.

Silas nodded in return. "Indeed."

Jenkins paused, allowing the corridor to play its part in the interaction.

"This will complicate things."

Silas responded as he always did when men attempted to frame consequences as warnings.

"Then perhaps things should have been easier from the start."

Jenkins studied him for a moment before continuing on his way.

Silas watched him leave.

It crossed his mind briefly that he was unsure if Jenkins genuinely believed his arguments. He suspected he did, in the way people believe in what keeps them employed and secure.

Silas turned back to Henry.

"We got it," Silas announced.

He awaited a sign — relief, gratitude, or at least a flicker of acknowledgment that they had pried something open. He was unaccustomed to working with clients who gauged outcomes differently than he did.

Henry merely stated, "Six months."

"Yes," Silas responded. "It's a foothold."

Henry's gaze drifted down the hall as if calculating distance.

"A foothold," Henry echoed, testing the phrase.

Silas noticed it but tried not to react.

***

The courthouse received Silas as it always had. Clerks nodded. Deputies greeted him with the familiarity earned over years of predictable behavior. No one asked what he was working on. That omission felt deliberate, though he could not yet prove it.

He spent the day observing patterns. Which filings moved quickly, and which ones stalled? Which names appeared repeatedly on internal memoranda? The machinery was not secretive. It was simply uninterested in retaliation.

Silas told himself he was doing what responsibility required. He was not provoking. He was not grandstanding. He was protecting his client by narrowing exposure.

Reducing harm, he believed, was not capitulation. It was opposition practiced patiently.

At lunch, he sat with men he had known for years. They spoke of standard matters, like budgets, judges, and an upcoming retirement.

When the conversation drifted toward recent developments in the capital, it did so indirectly. Phrases like *they're being careful up there* and *someone's decided to clean things up* passed without elaboration.

No one mentioned race.

That afternoon, Silas placed a call to a contact in Jackson, a man whose reliability rested entirely on keen ears and discretion. The line rang extended. When the man answered, his voice was deliberate and professional, almost detached.

"Yes," the man said, after Silas explained the nature of his inquiry. "I'm aware."

That was all.

Silas didn't press. Pressing created records, and records might require legal responses. Jackson specialized in responses that appeared unrelated to their causes.

He hung up and sat still, understanding now that the case had already been indexed – not by title, but by implication. No docket number existed yet. The system was alert to deviations long before they became formal.

Rather than alarm him, the realization steadied him. This was the environment he understood. Procedure and controlled movement.

It reassured him that he was operating within bounds.

That evening, Silas reviewed statutes governing jurisdiction, venue, and standing. He was not searching for leverage. He was identifying fault lines.

Outside, the town settled into itself. Lights appeared where expected. Traffic thinned on schedule. The quiet returned in increments.

Silas closed the book and turned off the lamp.

He told himself that nothing irreversible had begun.

He wanted to identify areas where discretion masqueraded as necessity. He marked passages where authority was described as customary or established practice. These phrases were not accidental. They allowed decisions to travel without attribution.

The District Courts favored language that could survive daylight.

Over the next several days, Silas altered his conduct in small, almost imperceptible ways. He documented everything privately. He refrained from committing strategy to paper. He understood that the earliest record of the case would not be his filings, but the system's internal assessments – quiet evaluations conducted by people whose names never appeared in opinions.

He received fewer calls than usual. That absence spoke clearly.

On Friday afternoon, he encountered a clerk he trusted – one of the few whose loyalty was to process rather than hierarchy. The clerk hesitated before speaking, then lowered his voice.

"Nothing official," the clerk said. "But things are being noticed."

Silas understood that was all that could be said.

The district court didn't intervene early. It waited until intervention appeared inevitable, then framed its involvement as stewardship rather than regulation. Silas understood now that the capital was not reacting to the case. It was preparing for its implications.

Saturday morning arrived quietly.

The mail came through the slot as it always did. The mailman knocked to let him know his postage had been successfully delivered. Silas waited before retrieving it; his new awareness of his surroundings required that he encounter it more deliberately.

The envelope was indistinguishable from the rest. No marking that would differentiate it from regular correspondence.

It was precisely what he had expected.

He separated it from the rest and placed it on the table. He didn't open it yet. Jackson never hurried. It assumed compliance would arrive on its own.

Silas understood then that the capital had already spoken, in words if not in posture. The letter was merely the formalization of a conversation already underway.

He finally reached for the envelope, not expecting any surprises.

The record, he knew, was being assembled elsewhere.

And soon, it would require his response.

Silas requested a bench trial after the final pretrial conference.

He framed the motion narrowly. Complexity. Judicial efficiency. The avoidance of confusion. He didn't mention representativeness. He didn't name what had already been settled.

The request sounded responsible. It presented itself as de-escalation. A way to spare the court unnecessary complication. A way to keep the matter within the clean lines of law rather than allowing it to wander into sentiment.

Silas believed, sincerely, that this would protect Henry.

Judge Mathewson reviewed the motion impassively.

He asked one question, procedural rather than probing whether both parties consented.

The State did.

Henry understood what the motion meant. Fewer eyes. Fewer voices. Less room for misinterpretation.

He also understood that an objection would look like distrust, so he remained silent.

The ruling arrived in writing the next day.

It was precise, nearly immaculate. The court found that the interests of justice would be best served by judicial determination. No commentary followed.

The decree didn't mention the jury that had already been shaped. It didn't need to. The mechanism was complete. What had been removed was not bias. It was friction.

Henry read the document, then set it aside.

He didn't read it again.

"They never were for us anyway," he said quietly.

Silas didn't respond.

Only after the order was entered did Silas allow himself to consider what had been preserved by its restraint. The law would speak now in a single voice. There would be no interruption. No dissent to absorb.

The clarity felt reassuring.

It should have alarmed him.

The clerk filed the order as a matter of routine.

Another case was called.

Nuremberg, Mississippi

ELEVEN AND ONE-HALF
Davis and Dillard

They exited together, not side by side, and not in public.

The courthouse steps were clean. The square was already returning to its usual rhythm, and nothing had yet been disrupted.

Silas watched Henry descend and step into the street with the same cautious demeanor he had adopted after jail, after warnings, after navigating the federal corridor. It wasn't meekness. It was a calculation.

Silas's car was parked on the north side.

Henry's truck was parked farther away, near the edge of downtown.

Henry reached the curb and paused.

"Mr. Thorn," he called.

Silas turned.

Henry didn't look up at him. He stared past him, toward the intersection.

"I'm going to stop by the supply store," Henry mentioned.

Silas frowned slightly. "Today?"

"Yeah, they told me my account was fine. I'm picking up what I need before the weekend."

Silas wanted to say something practical but lacked the words for what he felt.

"All right," he replied.

Henry finally looked at him for the first time since the ruling.

"You did what you said you would do."

To Silas, the statement felt oddly placed. It was neither praise nor affirmation – not the kind of confirmation that could later be used as evidence.

Henry turned and walked toward his truck.

Silas watched him blend into the routine traffic of the square.

Then Silas climbed into his car.

He drove back to his office and began drafting letters.

He penned one to the municipal clerk for the logs, another to the sheriff's department for supplementary records, and one to a county office that would claim it had no involvement in enforcement but would eventually produce a file.

His handwriting was neat. His language precise.

He hand-wrote the messages as if homespun gestures would compel compliance.

At noon, he ate at his desk. He didn't leave the office or go home.

He convinced himself he was simply busy.

At 2:40, his secretary knocked softly and entered without waiting for permission. Her expression was composed in a way Silas recognized: not fear, precisely, but the demeanor of someone delivering news that would chill the room.

"Mr. Thorn," she said, "Henry Logan is here."

Silas looked up. "Already?"

"He requested to see you."

Silas stood.

Henry entered the office and removed his hat, placing it on his knees as he always did. The gesture was so familiar that Silas felt, for a fleeting moment, reassured.

Then he noticed Henry's hands.

They were steadier than usual, which indicated he was deliberately controlling them.

Silas sat.

Henry hesitated before speaking.

He glanced at the corner of the desk, at the law books organized by usage, and at the nameplate Silas had once taken pride in but now avoided looking at directly.

"They closed my account," he stated.

"What do you mean?"

Henry's voice remained level. "The supply store. The one by Highway 41."

Silas leaned back, as if more distance could alter the meaning.

"They said it was a mistake," Silas said quickly, hearing the words spill out. "They…"

Henry shook his head.

"They said there was no mistake," he clarified. "They reviewed it this morning. They said they can't extend credit right now."

Silas felt irritation bubble up – at the store, at the timing, at the convenience of it all. He recognized the impulse and resented it because it sought a straightforward target for blame.

"That's… business," Silas said, still trying to frame it in familiar terms.

"Yes," Henry replied. "That's what they called it."

Silas's throat tightened.

"Do you have another supplier?"

"Not nearby."

Silas's mind raced, attempting to resolve a problem that was not meant to be resolved.

"I can call," Silas offered. "I know…"

Henry's hand lifted slightly, shaping the moment.

"It won't be you," he interjected softly.

The statement was calm and didn't assign blame. It did something worse: it defined the boundaries of Silas's power.

Silas sat in silence.

Henry continued.

"They didn't say it was because of the case," he explained. "They didn't mention you. They didn't mention the court. They didn't mention anything."

Silas nodded slowly.

Henry leaned forward.

"They said they were tightening," he asserted. "They said they needed to be cautious."

"And the contract?" Silas asked, already anticipating and dreading the answer.

Henry hesitated, looking down at his hat and adjusting the brim with his thumb.

"Mr. Dillard called."

Silas recognized the name – a man with properties on the west side, someone who acknowledged Silas at church.

Henry's voice remained steady.

"He said he's going to postpone the repairs. He said he's going to 'wait until things settle.'"

Silas felt a chilling realization.

"Did he explain why?" Silas asked, although he knew Dillard would never provide a reason.

"He didn't need to."

"Henry," he said cautiously, "this is retaliation."

Henry remained silent, allowing Silas to hear himself articulate it.

Silas continued, softer now.

"It's unlawful," he added, not that it made a difference.

Henry's stance didn't waver.

"It's not documented."

The motion had succeeded. The ruling had been granted. The law had functioned as it should within the confines of the courtroom.

Outside, the record didn't exist.

Silas's jaw tightened.

"You came to tell me," Silas said, almost instinctively.

"Yes."

"Why?" Silas asked.

Henry's response came without emphasis, as though it had been decided long before the question was posed.

"Because I wanted you to know," he said, "that you did what you said you would do."

Silas felt a shift within him.

Henry continued.

"And I wanted you to know that it still costs me."

There was no anger in his words.

Silas stared at him.

For the first time, the room felt more like a room than an office. The books seemed less like tools and more like furniture – objects arranged to imply competence.

At that moment, Henry had to admit that the summer he had envisioned was already behind him.

This was not due to any significant incident.

Instead, it was because uninterrupted days no longer existed.

Silas spoke thoughtfully, striving to keep the truth from becoming sentimental.

"I can help," he offered.

"You can help in court," Henry replied. "That's why I came."

Henry stood, placing his hat back on his head, and paused at the door, weighing whether anything else needed to be said.

Then he added, "They'll call it unfortunate. They'll label it business. That way, no one has to acknowledge what they're doing."

As Henry reached for the doorknob, he added, "And the worst part is that it will sound reasonable."

Silas remained seated. For a long moment, he didn't move. He was stunned, listening – listening to his own thoughts, trying to revert to doctrine, to procedure, to the comfort of a room that believed it could contain consequences.

His secretary passed by the doorway twice without glancing in.

Finally, Silas reached for a blank sheet of paper.

He wrote a single line at the top, slowly and deliberately, as if writing it could prevent it from occurring again.

Retaliation is not always illegal. Sometimes it is simply unrecorded.

He stared at the line.

Then, beneath it, he wrote a second line.

And the law, when it functions correctly, can make that easier.

He set the paper down.

For the first time since Henry had asked him to take the case, Silas Thorn comprehended something with clarity that didn't feel like anger and therefore could not be dismissed as "emotion."

He had secured a win in the only place the town was willing to be just.

And Henry had paid for it everywhere else.

Silas sat straight in his chair. He understood then that his carefulness – his moderation, his professionalism – was not a shield. It was a method. And it could be used against the very individual it claimed to protect.

He waited until evening.

The matter required time because it needed distance. Calls made too soon seemed reactive; calls made too late came across as calculated. He had learned – through years of observing men who survived longer than they deserved – that timing could be mistaken for virtue if executed correctly.

At 6:17 p.m., he dialed.

He didn't call Henry. He didn't call the supply store.

He called Mr. Dillard.

The number came to him effortlessly, which disturbed him. He had never saved it or written it down, but it resided among familiar names – alongside people who nodded at him in church, who pronounced "Silas" with the same intonation they used for safe or known.

The line rang twice.

"Dillard here."

"Tom," Silas said. "It's Silas Thorn."

A pause lingered – not startled, but one where a man recalibrates how to be heard.

"Well," Dillard finally replied, "that's a surprise."

"I won't keep you," Silas said. "I just wanted to address a minor matter."

He could already feel himself arranging the exchange to exit cleanly.

Dillard chuckled softly. "Of course."

Silas sat back in his chair, crossing one leg over the other.

"I understand you've postponed some repair work," Silas noted. "Work that Henry Logan was scheduled to complete."

Another pause, much longer and contemplative.

"Yes," Dillard confirmed. "That's correct."

"Henry's reliable. You know that."

"I do," Dillard replied easily. "He's always done good work."

Silas had anticipated resistance. In fact, he had prepared for it. What unsettled him was how unnecessary it proved.

"I was surprised," Silas continued, "that you'd hold off without cause."

Dillard exhaled slowly.

"Silas," he said, "there's no cause."

"That's exactly it," Silas replied, still not pushing. "It seemed... out of character."

Another small chuckle came from the other end.

"Look," Dillard said, "this isn't about Henry."

Silas felt exasperation wash over him and closed his eyes tightly.

"Then what is it about?" he asked.

The silence stretched long enough to feel useful.

"Things are unsettled," Dillard explained. "You know how that goes."

Silas felt something cold pass through him.

"I don't," he responded softly. "That's why I'm calling."

Dillard's tone shifted – not defensive, but faintly amused.

"You're in the middle of something," he said. "People notice."

Silas straightened.

"This is a legal matter," he asserted. "It's a question of ordinance enforcement."

Dillard laughed then, as if the word legal had arrived in a clown suit.

"Sure it is," he said. "In the courthouse."

Silas felt the distinction resonate.

"You're not suggesting," Silas began, then paused. He didn't want to provide Dillard with language he hadn't already claimed.

"I'm not suggesting anything," Dillard replied. "I'm merely saying it's not the right moment."

"For what?"

"For commitments. For changes. We don't need to be drawing attention."

"Henry's livelihood isn't attention," Silas argued. "It's work."

"I know," Dillard replied. "That's why I'm being cautious."

Cautious.

The term echoed in Silas's mind with a familiarity that made his stomach churn.

"Tom," Silas said, letting the name linger, "are you telling me you're punishing him?"

Dillard's response was immediate.

"No," he insisted. "Of course not. I'm postponing. That's not punishment. That's discretion."

Silas felt the last of his patience evaporate.

"Discretion exercised how?"

Dillard sighed – patient now, nearly indulgent.

"You've always been smart," he remarked. "You know how this town operates."

"I know how the law functions," he countered.

"Yes," Dillard confirmed. "And that's the issue."

Silas stared at the wall across from his desk – the same wall he had gazed at during countless phone calls that concluded with men thanking him for his reasonableness.

"What happens," Silas inquired, "if I insist?"

There was the test.

Dillard didn't hesitate.

"Then people will think you're confused," he replied. "Or worse – principled."

"And Henry?"

Dillard's voice cooled.

"Henry will be unfortunate," he said. "And everyone will feel bad about it."

"You're framing this as if it's neutral."

"It *is* neutral. It applies to everyone."

"Everyone who?"

Another pause ensued before Dillard answered carefully.

"Everyone who complicates things more than necessary."

Silas released a slow breath.

"I'm asking you to reconsider. Quietly."

Dillard laughed.

"Silas, you already asked loudly. You just didn't raise your voice."

The statement struck with surgical precision.

"I can't undo that," Dillard continued. "Neither can you."

Silas felt something within him fracture – not shatter or explode. Just misalign.

"So that's it?"

"Yes," Dillard affirmed. "For now."

Silas nodded, though Dillard could not see it.

"And later?"

Dillard's voice softened.

"Later," he said, "we'll all claim this was merely a rough patch. That cooler heads prevailed."

"And Henry?" Silas asked once more.

Dillard hesitated – not from doubt, but calculation.

"He'll adapt," he said. "They always do."

Silas remained silent.

"Well," Dillard added, brightening slightly, "I'm glad we spoke. It's good to clear the air."

"Yes," Silas replied.

The word felt insincere.

After the call ended, Silas remained standing.

He didn't sit. Standing felt more timely.

He approached the window and gazed at the streetlights. Evening had arrived unnoticed. Men crossed the street with the confidence of those who do not measure light. Storefronts glowed. Doors locked in expected order.

Silas realized then that nothing Dillard had said was illegal. Nothing had been threatened. Nothing had been promised. The call had been courteous and cooperative, even reasonable. That was what made it functional.

He returned to his desk and picked up the receiver again. This time, he dialed the supply store. The clerk answered on the third ring.

"Davis Hardware."

"This is Silas Thorn," he introduced himself. "I'd like to speak to the owner."

A pause followed. Papers rustled.

"I'm sorry," the clerk replied. "He's not available."

"May I leave a message?"

Another pause.

"I can," she said, "but I don't know that it will change anything."

"What will change it?" Silas asked.

The clerk lowered her voice slightly.

"Time," she replied. "Or forgetting."

"Forgetting what?"

The line went quiet.

Then, softly: "I don't know."

Silas hung up.

He sat at his desk and clasped his hands as judges did when they had finished listening.

Like Dillard, he had not threatened anyone, and he had not been threatened.

He had done precisely what was expected of him.

And in doing so, he grasped the final shape of the trap:

The law permitted him to speak.

Custom allowed others to respond.

And reasonableness ensured no one would ever label it as harm.

Silas reached for a legal pad and wrote a single sentence, as a record:

Complicity needs only fluency, not belief.

He tore the page off and placed it face down in the drawer with the case caption.

Then he turned off the light and left the office without locking the door.

He didn't anticipate anyone entering, but the system already had.

PART IV: ENDURANCE

TWELVE
Around the Clock Diner

By the time Robert Bullock found him, Silas had been awake long enough that he could not remember if it was Tuesday or Wednesday.

The truck stop diner sat beyond the county line, its neon sign flickering unevenly, deciding whether it could itself stay awake. It was the only place open at that hour. Everyone knew that, but no one admitted to relying on it.

Silas sat in a booth near the back, coffee untouched, cigarette burning down in the ashtray beside it, though he seldom smoked. He had ordered food, even though he had not intended to stay long.

The waitress had stopped asking questions after the second refill.

Bullock spotted him before Silas looked up. That, too, felt predictable.

Bullock paused inside the door, letting his eyes adjust. The place smelled of grease, long hauls, and fresh coffee – honest smells, he thought, though not comforting ones at the moment. He removed his hat and scanned the room once more.

Silas was hunched forward, forearms on the table, shoulders drawn in. The posture was wrong. Silas usually occupied space as if it had agreed to accommodate him.

Bullock slid into the booth across from him without asking.

Silas looked up, surprised, and then resigned.

"I didn't tell you where I was," Silas said.

"No," Bullock replied. "You told someone who knew where you'd go."

Silas flicked ash into the tray. "I wasn't hiding."

"No, you were waiting."

The waitress approached, pad already out. Bullock ordered black coffee without hesitation. She poured without attempting to make any small talk.

Silas stared into his cup. "You still think this is a mistake."

"Yes."

Silas smiled faintly. "Then you picked an odd night to come find me."

Bullock wrapped his hands around the mug, warming them. "Your assistant was concerned."

Silas's eyes widened. "She shouldn't be."

"She should," Bullock said. "That's why she's good."

Silas said nothing.

Outside, an 18-wheeler rumbled past, the sound low and constant, like Mississippi.

"They've stopped returning calls," Silas said finally. "Not all of them, just enough."

Bullock watched the steam rise from his coffee. "That's the first adjustment. It feels personal. It isn't."

Silas laughed quietly. "That's comforting."

Bullock retorted, "It's not meant to be."

They sat in silence for a moment. The diner was half-full – drivers eating slowly, a man asleep in a booth with his cap pulled low, two teenagers sharing fries and saying nothing. No one paid them any attention. That, Silas realized, was part of the appeal of this place.

"You could still step away," Bullock said. "Even now."

Silas shook his head. "No. That window closed earlier than I expected."

Bullock nodded, confirming a calculation he had already made.

"I thought so," he said.

Silas looked up. "Then why come?"

Bullock took a sip from his mug. Though it was bad, he drank it anyway.

"Because when men decide they can't go back, they tend to make other mistakes. They stop sleeping. They stop eating. They start mistaking determination for clarity."

Silas glanced down at the untouched plate in front of him. He had not remembered ordering it.

"I'm not asking you to agree," Bullock continued. "I'm not asking you to help."

Silas raised an eyebrow. "You tracked me to a truck stop at midnight to say that?"

Bullock allowed himself the smallest smile. "I'm asking you not to disappear."

The words hit harder than Bullock intended. Silas's expression shifted – not breaking, but tightening, as if something had been worn down.

"They'll come after Henry," Silas said. "You know that."

"Yes."

"And after me."

"Yes."

Silas stared at the window, at the reflection of neon bleeding into the dark. "Then you should keep your distance."

Bullock leaned in. "I won't."

"That's not wise."

"No," Bullock agreed. "But it's accurate."

Another truck passed. The waitress refilled their cups without asking.

"I don't have your appetite for this kind of exposure," Bullock said. "I never have, but I can sit in a diner at midnight and make sure you eat something."

Bullock slid the untouched plate closer. 'Start there.'

Silas picked up the fork.

They didn't speak while he ate.

Bullock watched the room – not anxiously, attentively. When Silas finished, Bullock stood and put on his hat.

"I'll check in tomorrow," he said. "If you're not at your office, I'll know where to look."

"You don't have to do this."

Bullock paused at the end of the booth. "I know."

He left a few bills on the table – more than was needed – and walked out into the dark.

Silas sat for a long moment after he was gone. The diner looked the same as before, but he felt something shift.

When the waitress returned, Silas ordered another plate – this one hot – and ate it slowly, knowing the night was no longer something he could simply wait out.

THIRTEEN
The Language Fails

Preparing for the case forced Henry and Silas to be together more than either was comfortable.

They liked each other well enough. Not well enough to be friends, and not well enough to pretend this was anything other than necessity.

By the time Henry arrived at Silas's Greenville office, it was about 4 p.m., so he knew he could not stay more than an hour. The street below had begun to thin, the ordinary certainty that nothing would disturb the evening.

They worked in silence longer than expected. Legal pads accumulated Silas's thoughts as notes. The air in the room grew heavy with the unspoken understanding that neither man would leave until something unresolved forced itself into the open.

Greenville had taught Silas that the law worked best when it was rarely questioned.

"Henry," he said, carefully, "can I ask you something that might be a little uncomfortable?"

Henry didn't look up.

"Don't you always?"

Silas exhaled, as though he hadn't thought of it that way.

"Well, I hope not. But I suppose I haven't given that much consideration."

"Go ahead."

Silas hesitated long enough to convince himself he was being thoughtful.

"Why do Negroes commit so many crimes?"

Henry froze – not theatrically, but obviously annoyed. He leaned back; eyes fixed somewhere above Silas's head, as though an acceptable answer might be suspended in the air.

"What Negroes are you referring to?" Henry asked finally.

Silas shrugged.

"I don't know. Not all, obviously. But more than half, wouldn't you say?" He leaned forward instead of retreating, mistaking projection for courage.

Henry's voice was steady when he replied.

"I'm not violent. I've never committed what I consider a real crime – unless you count being in the wrong place at the wrong hour. My record does. I don't."

Silas recognized that this confirmed something rather than complicated it.

"When I think I can begin to trust you," Henry said, in a voice a little louder than normal, "you say something racist."

"That's exactly my point," Silas replied, relieved to have reached what he believed was common ground. "In court, the defense will argue that rigid enforcement is necessary because Negroes pose a threat. They'll bait you and provoke you. Everyone will be watching to see if you respond the way a normal man would."

Henry looked directly at him now.

"You can't afford to do that," Silas continued. "You have to be… abnormally controlled."

"And what," he asked, "do I say that you consider to be racist?" Silas frowned, genuinely puzzled.

"You called me 'one of the good ones.' You described James Baldwin as 'angry.' Those are the kinds of words White people use when they believe they're being factual instead of judgmental."

Silas listened and didn't interrupt.

"Are you sure you aren't just… being overly sensitive," he asked cautiously.

Henry's chair scraped softly as he leaned forward.

"I've been a Negro my entire life," he said. "I know the pattern. I know the terms. The same way I know the pattern of unequal enforcement in this state."

The bluntness caught Silas's attention.

"Fair point. I'll try to be more careful what I say moving forward."

The light outside the window had shifted. Henry noticed. Silas didn't.

Silas cleared his throat.

"How's your family holding up? Do you need anything?"

The question struck Henry differently than intended.

"I need work," Henry said. The words came quicker than he meant them to. "I've had jobs here and there, but nothing steady. I need work, man."

Silas nodded again, already calculating solutions that didn't require discomfort.

"I don't have a long-term answer, but I do have some things around the house I've been putting off," Silas said. "I could pay you. I'll be home all day Saturday."

"I'm free most days," he said. "Why wait until Saturday?"

"It's the only day I'll be home this week."

Henry considered him for a moment.

"You could leave the key and instructions," he offered. "It'll be done before you get home. It's not as though I haven't been inside your house before."

Silas shifted.

"I don't know," he said. "Let me think about it."

Henry stood. He understood the answer immediately.

"Never mind," he said. "I'll be there at eight Saturday morning."

"Alright," Silas replied, unaware of what he had inadvertently confirmed. "I'll see you then."

Henry stepped into the hallway and shook his head before putting his hat back on.

This was going to be a difficult lesson for Silas Thorn to learn. He didn't yet see how often he repeated the very thing he claimed to oppose.

Henry took the stairs instead of the elevator. In that old building, he didn't have time to waste waiting for the elevator.

Offices were already closing, doors slamming shut and lights going out in a routine so familiar it could have been staged. Greenville knows how to finish the day without calling attention to itself.

Outside, the street had fallen into its evening posture. A driver passed, inattentive to the fading sunlight. A woman locked the door of the pharmacy across the way and didn't look up as Henry stepped onto the sidewalk.

He checked his watch.

Plenty of time, or, at least, enough time to get home. The difference mattered.

As he walked, he replayed the conversation without any anger. What he felt instead was recognition – the familiar burden of having explained something carefully to someone who believed caring was the same thing as understanding.

Behind him, Silas's office light remained on.

By the time he reached the corner, the street behind him had gone quiet, as it always did. Greenville settling back into the certainty that it would not be asked to account for itself tonight.

Henry adjusted his hat and kept walking.

Nuremberg, Mississippi

FOURTEEN
Go the Distance

Henry arrived at Silas's house at 7:48 a.m. Silas had already been awake for nearly an hour.

He stood at the kitchen window with a cup of coffee that had long since stopped steaming, watching the road with the vague justification that he was waiting on a man who had already proven himself punctual. The house was quiet in the way it always was on Saturdays — no hearings, no calls, and no expectation that the day would demand more than he chose to give it.

Henry parked where the gravel drive widened, careful not to block the mailbox. Silas noticed the precision and dismissed it as coincidence. The truck was older but well kept.

Henry checked his watch before stepping out.

Silas opened the door before Henry reached the porch to avoid standing there wondering what it would mean to wait.

"Morning," Silas said.

"Morning," Henry replied.

They didn't shake hands.

Inside, the house felt unchanged – cool and familiar. Shoes lined by the door. A jacket hung where it had been placed and forgotten. Silas gestured toward the kitchen.

"I wrote a list," he said. "Nothing major."

He didn't ask where to begin.

Silas watched as Henry set his toolbox down carefully, controlling the sound. This was Silas's house. The awareness didn't need to be stated.

"Coffee?" Silas asked.

"No, thank you."

They walked through the house together at first. Silas pointed out a loose hinge, a warped section of fence visible through the back window, a cracked garage pane that had gone long enough without demanding attention to feel permanent. Each explanation assumed permanence that the house would remain exactly where it was, intact and unquestioned.

Henry listened without comment.

By 8:10, the tour had ended. Silas lingered in the kitchen doorway, uncertain what his presence now required. He had insisted on being home. He had not decided what that meant.

"Well," he said finally, "I'll be around."

Henry went straight to work.

Silas retreated to the living room. Legal papers lay folded beside him on the couch, the television dark. He told himself he was reviewing notes. What he was doing instead was listening – counting the rhythm of repairs, the restraint of sound, the absence of excess motion.

This was not supervision. It felt closer to habit than choice.

Silas remained seated, increasingly aware that the only man in the house who appeared fully at ease was the one he had insisted on watching.

A hinge squeaked one more time. Then stopped.

"You don't need to be quiet," Silas said, raising his voice enough to carry. "It's my house."

There was a pause before Henry answered.

"I know," he said. "Old habit."

Silas said he understood.

Outside, a lawnmower started two houses down. Somewhere else, a screen door opened and closed. The neighborhood performed its Saturday rituals, undisturbed.

Silas picked up the legal papers and unfolded them. He read the first paragraph twice without absorbing it. The words felt oddly light, as though they were already moving ahead of him.

He stood and drifted into the kitchen, leaning against the counter. Henry was finishing the repair at the back door. The hinge closed cleanly now, no longer making a statement.

"You've done this a lot," Silas said.

Henry tested the door once more.

"Enough."

Silas hesitated.

"You could've waited until I was gone," he said. "I told you I'd be home, but ..."

He stopped, unable to complete the thought without naming it.

"You asked me to come when you were here," Henry said. Not defensive. Not accusatory. Just factual.

Silas felt a tightening in his chest.

"Yes," he said. "I did."

They stood there silent.

"Fence is next," Henry said.

Silas stepped aside.

In the backyard, the oak tree cast a wide shadow across the grass. The fence leaned enough to suggest neglect. Henry knelt, tested the post carefully, and applied pressure in increments.

"You don't have dogs," Henry said.

"No."

"Kids?"

"No."

Henry stayed focused on why he was there.

Silas stood on the porch, arms folded, watching. He noticed – without knowing why – that Henry positioned himself so he never disappeared from view, never fully leaving the line of sight from the house.

Silas told himself this was courtesy.

When the fence held firm again, Silas stepped down and tested it himself, pressing harder than he thought it might need to withstand in a storm.

"Good," he said. "Good work."

Inside again, Silas poured fresh coffee, then stopped before offering it. He drank it himself, standing at the sink.

"You ever think about taking on less dangerous work?" he asked. "Something steadier?"

Henry considered this.

"Dangerous for who?" he asked.

Silas opened his mouth, then closed it.

"I know what you mean," Henry added.

The garage window was last. Henry removed the broken pane carefully, set the glass aside, and fitted the replacement cleanly. He wiped away excess putty until the surface looked untouched.

Silas leaned closer to the finished pane.

"That crack had been there so long," he said, "I stopped noticing it."

Henry packed his tools.

"That happens," he said. "People stop seeing what stays broken."

Silas reached into his pocket and produced the envelope he had prepared the night before. He handed it over.

Henry accepted it without counting.

"Thank you," he said.

Silas hesitated.

"You don't have to be so careful here," he said.

"I know where I am," Henry said. "That's how I work."

Henry put on his hat and headed for the door. Silas followed him to the porch.

The neighborhood looked unchanged, reconciled and untouched by what had occurred inside the house.

"I'll see you Monday," Henry said.

"Yes," Silas replied. "Monday."

Henry drove away.

Silas remained on the porch, hands in his pockets, listening as the sound of the truck faded and the morning resumed its practiced calm.

Only much later would he understand that this had been the moment.

Not when the case was argued.

Not when the ruling came.

But when a man had been in his house, repaired what he had overlooked, moved through the space without ever being allowed to forget it was not his – and left everything intact.

Including the distance.

Nuremberg, Mississippi

FIFTEEN
Getting a Lifeline

The Tip Top Club was present before it appeared. Delta blues spilled into the street, a Stratocaster bending a note around the corner, conversation settling into rhythm behind it. Henry slowed down so Silas could hear.

"This place is all right," Henry said.

It was September 8 – Henry's 30th birthday – and Silas made the offer to take him anywhere he wanted to go and foot the bill.

To his surprise, Henry not only accepted, but he saw an opening to expose Silas to his world on a friendly basis.

Inside, the light was low and forgiving. Tables crowded close to the bandstand, their occupants leaning forward as if proximity could deepen the musical experience. It was not a place to be seen. It was a place to be safely present.

Henry instinctively knew where to stand – not too close to the door, and not too close to the bar. He guided Silas toward a narrow stretch beside a column where the crowd naturally parted and re-formed, like water around stone.

"You come here often?" Silas asked.

Henry smiled. "Often enough to know when not to."

Silas took that in. He had learned that Henry's sentences usually carried a second meaning, and that it was better to wait than to ask.

A woman approached. Early thirties, confident, luminous. She didn't look at Silas.

"You're Henry Logan," she said. "The one fighting Mississippi."

"That's me. But I'm not here to be noticed."

"You dance?"

Henry smiled. "No. I'm married."

She laughed. "That wasn't the question."

She turned to Silas for the first time, assessing him briefly. She tilted her head toward the bandstand.

"Does your friend dance?"

Silas froze. This was not a courtroom pause. No objection to raise. No rule to consult. A room full of witnesses who had not been told they were watching.

"He might if he's invited," Henry said, mischievously.

The woman extended her hand. "I'm inviting."

Silas hesitated, then laughed quietly at himself and removed his jacket.

"I should warn you," he said, standing. "I argue better than I move."

She smiled. "That makes two of us."

As they stepped onto the floor, Henry stayed where he was. He didn't follow with his eyes. That was courtesy. He knew the rules of such things.

A moment later, someone took the empty space beside him. A man stood calmly, his attention directed toward the band, though he didn't seem entirely engrossed by their performance.

"Good place," the man said.

Henry recognized the voice before the face confirmed it.

"Yes, sir."

"I hear it stays that way because people protect it," the man said. "Carefully."

They stood together while the music did its work. On the floor, Silas moved stiffly at first, then less so. He was concentrating – not on rhythm, but on not being afraid to relax. Henry noticed.

The man beside him glanced over. "Your friend looks like someone learning where he's allowed to belong."

Henry allowed himself a small smile. "He's been learning that his whole life. He's new to rooms like this."

"Some lessons travel better than others," the man said.

When the song ended, Silas returned, flushed and faintly astonished.

"Thank you," he said to Henry – not for the dance, but for the initiative that had made it possible.

Henry smiled. "I'm impressed. I didn't think you would do it."

Silas glanced toward the bandstand, then back. "That man looks familiar. Do you know him?"

"Not personally," Henry said. "But yes."

They stayed until the music slowed and the room began to empty. When they left, Silas didn't ask questions. That, too, was trust.

Outside, the night had not changed, but something between them had.

Henry suggested one more stop while they were still on this side of town.

The Alamo held light rather than projecting it. A simple marquee with hand-set letters. Sound moved outward along Farish Street, footsteps pacing the sidewalk with purpose. This was not refuge. It was continuity.

Inside, the theater had been altered for the evening. The front rows were empty, the stage pulled forward to host a small ensemble – piano, upright bass, and brushed drums. The screen behind them caught the smoke and shadows. The music moved intentionally, aware of where it was.

Silas noticed the Negro Motorist Green Book near the lobby desk before anything else.

It lay open, Jackson listings already familiar to most who passed. The Alamo was there in plain type. Not emphasized. Simply present. That was its protection.

They sat along the side wall, Henry choosing the chair that faced the door.

James Baldwin arrived between sets.

Silas nudged Henry. "Is that James Baldwin?"

Henry smiled. "The same one you missed at the Tip Top. I guess the lighting is better here."

The owner greeted Baldwin quietly, accustomed to unassuming notices. Baldwin's jacket was dark. His attention immediate.

"You pick good places," Baldwin said, sitting.

"They've seen what lasts."

They spoke beneath the music – about ordinances that never named race, about curfews enforced through discretion, about how a man could comply fully and still be found in violation.

Silas listened. Baldwin watched him listening.

"This case," Baldwin said finally, "will cost you before it convinces anyone."

Silas didn't object.

Baldwin removed an envelope from his jacket and placed it on the table.

"This place stays open," he said, "because someone once decided it mattered whether Negro people had somewhere to arrive intact."

He looked at Henry.

"This money exists for the same reason."

Henry didn't touch it.

"It's not charity," Baldwin added. "It's insulation. So the truth doesn't retreat before it's heard."

The music ended. Applause rose – measured and satisfied.

Baldwin stood and disappeared back into the room, leaving the envelope where it lay.

Henry picked it up only after he was gone.

"This buys us time," he said.

Silas shook his head. "It buys us the chance to last."

At the bar, Henry greeted a wiry man with a bright tie and watchful eyes.

"Evenin', Brother."

"Evenin'. You here because you wanted to be, or because you needed to be?"

"Sometimes that's the same thing."

"I saw who you came in with."

"He's looking for a way to leave whole."

"That something you can give him?"

Henry breathed in slowly. "I know the door."

"Careful," the man said. "Some doors lock behind you."

Henry's mouth tightened. Almost a smile. "That's why I keep a foot in the frame."

The man raised his glass. "Storm don't like being named."

"Storm only matters if we stay outside."

They parted with a brief embrace.

Silas stood nearby, close enough to hear every word, and still, not understanding any of it.

On the sidewalk, the street cooled.

"That man at the bar," Silas said. "What were you talking about?"

Henry stopped.

"Nothing," he said. Then, "nothing you needed to worry over."

"It sounded...coded."

Henry studied him.

"In this state," he said, "we learn to talk in ways that won't get us killed. Even when it's just us."

"I heard every word," Silas said.

Henry knew Silas needed a cultural translation. "Hearing isn't the same as standing inside it."

They waited as a car passed.

"People like us," Henry added, circling his hand as if he was drawing a boundary around this section of Jackson, "we live near doors we can't always open. Storms we can't always outrun. We plan so we can get home."

Silas absorbed that.

"And you walking through that door tonight," Henry said quietly, "that's why folks were watching. Everybody was deciding what weather you were."

Silas searched for an answer and found only honesty.

"I don't know," he said.

Henry understood.

"Most storms don't."

SIXTEEN
The Morning After

Silas woke before the sun did. That, more than anything, surprised him.

He had expected the events of the night to pin him down, but instead he rose with a mind already moving, restless and disoriented, but startlingly exhilarating. The ceiling fan continued its deliberate pace above him, blades whispering in circles. For a moment he lay still, unsure whether he was awake or simply thinking too loudly.

His body ached from the tension he had carried. He sat up slowly, pressing his palms against his knees, breathing deeply through a smile that surprised him.

Nuremberg, Mississippi

He sat on the edge of the bed before standing again. The knee protested – not sharply, but enough to insist on a reaction. It always did after long hours or too much walking. Or dancing.

He pressed his thumb into the joint, feeling for the familiar throbbing. The doctors, years ago, had chosen their words carefully. Nothing catastrophic. Nothing repairable either. One bad collision in a game that should not have mattered stopped a season midway.

There had been interest before that. Letters, conversations, men who watched from the stands and spoke in conditions rather than commitments. He had not understood at the time how narrow the interval was. Only that it seemed open – until it wasn't.

He had finished school because there was nothing else to finish. Baseball didn't end dramatically; it simply declined to continue. The body unilaterally made the decision without asking about his plans.

Years later, the knee still served as a record of that refusal. Not a warning, nor a punishment – a little reminder of how quickly a future could be withdrawn once it became inconvenient to maintain.

Reflex normally dictated his morning: shower, shave, coffee, review notes, read a newspaper he pretended not to care about. Today, none of that arrived in order.

He splashed water on his face at the basin, watching his reflection in the frosty mirror. His eyes were clearer than they were yesterday, as though knowledge itself had hindsight. He lingered there.

His suit still lay on the chair where he had abandoned it. Wrinkled and improper. A detail that would normally needle him into fixing it. Instead, he stared at the fabric and remembered the faint echo of last night's smoke and perfume.

He found himself pacing. Five steps from bathroom door to window, five steps back. At the window, he pushed the curtains aside with two fingers. Daylight was not yet fully formed, for now still a pale orange rim on the horizon.

Jackson was quiet, the street below empty except for one man setting out folding chairs outside his small store preparing for his business day. Silas watched the man's unhurried movements and wondered if routine, too, was a kind of armor.

The law no longer felt like the first thing. It was still necessary, but he sensed that something else acted as its companion.

He made the bed. That surprised him as well. He tucked corners precisely, smoothing blankets with the kind of care he typically reserved for professional spaces. It was as though imposing order inside the room might prevent disorder inside himself.

In the small lobby downstairs, the clerk nodded at him. A White man at least twenty years his senior. Silas waited for his own expression to reveal something – shame, guilt, or defiance – yet found nothing on his face. The detachment startled him. Perhaps that, too, was change.

"Coffee?" the clerk asked.

Silas motioned toward the cup as he began refilling. He wrapped his hands around the cup, letting the heat inhabit his fingers. He drank it slowly. It grounded him.

He found himself searching the lobby for a newspaper, carrying reflexive curiosity about whether the Tip Top Club had somehow followed him into print. Absurd, he knew, and yet he checked.

The headlines spoke of rain, politics, a cotton shortage, and some other things he barely noticed. Nothing of smoke-filled rooms, or men who wrote like prophets, or envelopes holding a second chance and condemnation at once.

Nothing of a woman with a red ribbon who had taken his hand as if it were the most natural thing in the world.

He walked outside. The air was crisp in a way Mississippi mornings rarely were. He stood on the steps, coffee cooling in his hand, unsure where to go. For the first time in memory, the courthouse was not his automatic destination.

He thought of Henry. Of what Henry might already be doing – tending to his family, or standing in his yard barefoot before the pressure of the moment reintroduced itself. Silas wondered if Henry had slept, or if the night had changed him too, but in a way that didn't require explanation.

Silas looked down at his shoes. Dust from the Tip Top floor still clung to the leather. He almost bent to wipe it away. Almost. Then he chose not to.

A small, unspoken decision. Nothing dramatic, but another in a series of noticeable turning points.

In a couple of days, he would meet up with Henry again. They would return to work. The trial awaited with its motions, risks, and expectations still fully intact.

But Silas knew this now, the story he was fighting had already begun to rewrite him.

As the sun crawled fully over the buildings, casting a clean band of light across the steps, Silas stepped forward, cooling coffee in one hand, noticeable dust on his shoes, and let the day come to him instead of running ahead to meet it.

He didn't go searching for the Tip Top Club again later that morning. He was unfamiliar with Jackson from a bird's eye view, so after leaving the hotel, his feet waywardly carried him toward Farish Street. The city moved differently in the daylight. Vendors setting up crates, the slow shuffle of capitalism gaining momentum, the muted clang of a shopkeeper raising a metal grate. Farish Street – alive last night with guitars and night moves – was now stripped to its bones.

It made the night feel like something he had imagined.

He was about to turn back when he saw her, standing outside a storefront two doors down from the Tip Top. She was folding linens into a wooden crate – so carefully and methodically, she seemed choreographed. Her red ribbon was gone. Her hair, now loose, pinned simply at the sides. Without the music, she seemed smaller and quieter than his imagination. She was merely an extraordinary human again.

Silas froze where he stood, uncertain whether he was meant to speak. She looked up before he could decide.

"You're back," she said.

Her voice was gentle, but she didn't smile. That absence of emotion made the remark feel like a statement rather than an accusation.

"I was just out for a walk," Silas replied. It sounded inadequate even to him.

"You don't live here," she said. It was an observation, not a question.

"No," he admitted.

She finished placing one last folded cloth into the crate before straightening. In daylight, her eyes were daring. Not unfriendly, but no longer offering guidance the way they had last night on the dance floor.

"You danced," she said, wiping her hands on her apron. "That surprised me."

"It surprised me, too."

A moment of silence emerged between them – sufficiently significant to allow either party to depart, yet subtle enough that both chose to remain.

He cleared his throat. "I realized we never exchanged names."

"Most people here don't give theirs to strangers," she answered.

"I won't use it for anything," he said too quickly. "I only ..."

She tilted her head, studying him. "You think a name is a harmless thing?"

He didn't know how to answer that. The law taught him those names – on filings, sworn statements, court captions – were anything but harmless.

Still, he waited.

"My name is Lorraine," she said at last. "Lorraine Bishop."

She offered it as though it were a risk.

He was stunned. "Lorraine was my mother's name. I'm Silas. Nice to meet you, Lorraine."

She repeated it softly to test the shape of it. "Silas. That sounds like a name with history."

"My father chose it," he said. "And his father before him." He didn't explain what that lineage meant, and she didn't ask.

She lifted the crate and placed it inside the doorway. When she came back, she noticed the dust on his shoes.

"You kept it," she said.

"What?"

"The dust." She pointed lightly. "Most men of your stature would've cleaned themselves before leaving the hotel."

He looked down again. He had forgotten. "I haven't had time."

"You had time," she corrected softly. "You made a choice."

He felt himself blush.

"Why were you there?" he asked. "Last night."

"Because music makes us feel like people," she said. "Even when the world insists we're something else."

He didn't expect an answer like that. It struck him like a truth punch from a professional boxer.

"And you?" she asked. "Why were you there?"

He wanted to say something clever. Something true. Something that matched the solemnity of her question.

Instead, what came was: "Because I didn't know I wasn't allowed to be."

Her expression barely changed. Something like a cross between pity and a warning flickered across her face.

"You know now," she said.

"Yes."

"And you're here anyway."

"Yes."

Another break. The morning sounds filled it – shop shutters opening, distant church bells, a boy jumping rope somewhere on the next street.

She stepped aside, giving him room to stand closer if he chose. He didn't.

"You should go," she said, her voice free of rejection, simply recognizing the reality they both understood.

Silas drew a breath. "Will I see you again?"

"That depends," she said. "Night is one world. Day is another. Most men don't cross both."

He accepted the phrasing without fully understanding.

"Thank you," she said softly.

"For what?"

"For the dance," she answered. "And for not pretending it didn't happen."

Silas smiled as he lowered his eyes.

"Goodbye, Silas."

"Goodbye… Lorraine."

He turned, walking back toward the main street. He did look over his shoulder and felt the moment settling inside him, quiet as the dust on his shoes, yet permanent as a familiar name.

Nuremberg, Mississippi

- 150 -

SEVENTEEN
Muscle Shoals

Silas didn't tell anyone where he was going. That alone told him the trip mattered.

He left Jackson before dawn, the inside of the courthouse still dark, the square still empty. The car radio crackled between stations until he found a weak signal carrying a soul record he didn't recognize. The singer's voice was raw and unpolished, the kind that assumed the listener would lean in rather than be impressed. Silas kept it there.

He had heard the name Rick Hall the night before in a diner conversation he hadn't meant to overhear. Two men at the counter, both White, both in work shirts, talking about Muscle Shoals the way people talked about Canada during the war — like a rumor that had become inconveniently real.

"They don't even separate 'em," one of them said, not angry so much as confused. "They just play."

Silas paid his check and drove home, thinking about that sentence. By midnight, he was packing a change of clothes and folding his case notes into the glove compartment as if it were a bank vault.

The road northeast leveled and then ascended again, pine and red clay giving way to something softer. Nothing changed as he crossed into Alabama, except his expectation.

Muscle Shoals didn't make a public announcement. It sat low and plain, like a village created to avoid attention. Silas drove by the studio once before realizing he had arrived. There is no symbol that claims transformational.

Inside, the building smelled like life, similar to the Jackson clubs he had visited earlier in the week. The walls here were lined with instruments that looked used rather than displayed. A man with a cigarette behind his ear stood near the soundboard, listening to a playback with his eyes closed.

"You lost?" the man asked, without opening them.

Silas introduced himself and gave his name without the title. The man nodded, filing it away for later use.

"I'm Rick," he said. "You drove a long way to be standing in that doorway."

Silas told him the truth, or enough of it. That he was a lawyer. That he was trying a case that had begun to feel larger than the courthouse meant to hold. That he had heard about this place and needed to see it before he could decide whether he believed it.

Rick Hall laughed.

"Most folks come here trying to figure out how it works," he said. "They don't usually admit they're trying to believe."

They sat on folding chairs near the wall while a session reset itself. A Negro drummer tapped lightly on the rim of his snare, testing the room. A White guitarist tuned and retuned, not looking at anyone in particular. No one asked where anyone else stood.

Rick spoke in sentences that stayed close to the ground.

"I didn't set out to integrate anything," he said. "I set out to make records. Turns out, if you want the best sound, you don't get to choose the color."

Silas watched the room as Rick talked. There were no speeches. No posted rules or orders that needed to be enforced.

"You don't get much trouble?" Silas asked.

Rick shrugged. "Plenty of folks don't like it. But here's the thing – they don't feel accused. They feel left out. And that's different."

That sentence stayed between them longer than the music.

Silas told him about the case then. About Mississippi. About how every filing, every argument, no matter how careful, seemed to harden the people he needed to reach. Judges became defensive. Clerks retreated into preordered roles. Even allies spoke more quietly, worried that proximity itself was dangerous.

"Let's go to lunch and talk some more," Rick interrupted. "There are some things I want you to fully understand about what lessons I've had to learn the hard way."

When Rick pushed open the door of the catfish restaurant – whitewashed exterior, Coca-Cola sign bolted above the awning – Silas thought for half a second that he had walked into a place his father might have taken him on a long drive through Tennessee. Wood-paneled walls. Tin signs advertising gasoline brands that no longer existed. A fish mounted over the counter, its expression permanently surprised.

Rick confidently led the way. His son – five-year-old Rick Jr. – came bounding behind, one palm pressed to his father's thigh. The hostess, who seemed to recognize them immediately, handed them three menus without asking.

"We'll take the usual," Rick said, not even sitting before he spoke. "Three plates. One without the hushpuppies." He gestured toward his son. "He won't touch 'em. Claims they look like fishing bait."

Rick Jr. swung his legs under the table once seated, heels tapping chair rungs with restless energy. He stared openly at Silas.

"You're a lawyer," he announced, not as a question as much as a discovery.

Silas smiled, unsure what to say to a child who had made the proclamation. "That's what they call me, yes."

"What do you do?" the boy asked.

Rick answered for him. "He fights with paper instead of fists."

Silas let out a quiet breath through his nose – half amusement, half agreement. "That is close enough."

The boy was satisfied with this mystery. Then his attention shifted.

"What's Vanderbilt?" he asked, tasting the syllables. "Is that a ship?"

Silas blinked. Rick raised his eyebrows, waiting. They didn't realize Ricky had been listening to their exchange in the car.

Silas said slowly, "It's the name of a school."

Rick Jr. beamed with reverence, as though Silas had said the word playground.

"I like that name," the boy whispered. "Vander-bilt." He repeated it, as though it were a magic summons, and Silas felt some strange burden – unearned, unwanted – land on him. The boy believed the world was understandable by naming it.

The waitress set down sweet tea in sweating glasses. Rick rested his elbows on the table.

"You came all the way down here," Rick began, "because you heard a rumor. That I'm running a business where White and Black folks sit at the same table, play the same music, and leave the same door as equals."

"It's more than a rumor," Silas said quietly. "The area of the country you and I share believes there is a specific way of doing things. That some are meant to abide, and others to command. I need to know how you broke that rule without paying a price."

Rick chuckled, not cruelly, but knowingly. "You think I haven't paid? Every time a man with power hears my name, he remembers what I've done. And he hates that I did it without his permission." He took a slow drink, then continued. "What you want isn't easy, Counselor. You want Mississippi to feel indicted without admitting it's the defendant."

Silas was beginning to understand.

"That's what I learned in the studio," Rick said. "If I tell a man his voice is wrong, he'll harden. If I tell him the room is wrong, the microphone, the angle – he'll try again. Folks fight to protect their pride. Not the truth. Pride is the altar."

Silas's pulse quickened, though his face remained composed.

"So, you're saying …"

"I'm not saying stop suing Mississippi," Rick cut in. "I'm saying pay attention to what you're actually suing – the thing that made Mississippi possible."

Silas felt the sentence reverberate in him as a chord played cleanly on a guitar string.

"Systems don't have pride," Rick said. "Men do. If you name a system the enemy, men can watch the battle without feeling attacked. Give them distance, and they'll hear you. Push them into the ring, and they'll swing before you even raise a hand."

The waitress delivered plates piled high with fried catfish, coleslaw, hushpuppies, and tartar sauce in small paper cups. Rick Jr. immediately picked up a piece of catfish with both hands, ignoring utensils.

Silas didn't lift his fork.

He stared instead at the condensation on his glass.

"You look like someone handed you a verdict," Rick observed.

"Because I think they have."

Rick's tone changed as he watched Silas absorb the advice.

"You want to win," he said. "But winning ain't the same as changing. What I'm saying is, whatever you decide to do, make sure you can live with the outcome."

Rick Jr. had sauce on his cheeks when he spoke again. "When I grow up, I want to be a lawyer."

Silas almost laughed. But instead, he felt an unexpected sense of grief. He knew a five-year-old could say such a sentence naturally. And a five-year-old growing up in Mississippi on the wrong side of its lines might never dare to.

He finally reached for his fork, then put it back down.

"If Little Ricky can eat with his hands, I can too," Silas said, returning the sense of awe.

After lunch and a brief shift in topics, they headed back to FAME Studios to continue Rick's assignment.

Silas thought of the courtroom. Of men who insisted they were not cruel because cruelty required intent. Of laws that claimed to balance the way this room claimed acoustics.

"You're saying I should stop naming the state," Silas said.

"I'm saying stop giving them a mirror," Rick replied. "Give them a diagram."

On the drive back home, Silas didn't turn on the radio. He replayed the conversation instead, testing it for weakness. The idea felt dangerous in a new way.

Mississippi had always been the defendant because "Mississippi" could argue back.

A system could not take offense. It could only be exposed.

By the time he crossed the state line again, the sun was setting. Silas slowed, not out of caution, but recognition. He understood now that what Rick had built in Muscle Shoals was not defiance. It was inevitability.

The sound had slipped the line because it had refused to acknowledge the line.

Silas pulled over to the shoulder of the highway, long enough to write two brief sentences in the margin of his notes:

Do not prosecute a place. Prosecute the machinery that makes the place possible.

He closed the notebook and drove on, already rehearsing how he would say it aloud – calmly and carefully – until it sounded less like an accusation and more like the truth people had been waiting to hear.

- 158 -

EIGHTEEN
The Caption

They were in Silas's office again, late afternoon, same room where Henry had once sat stiff and guarded, unsure whether this native could carry a case that could break his own state.

Silas had been pacing, a habit he despised in others but permitted in himself. Henry sat near the window, hat in his lap, elbows on knees. The silence felt full, as though each was waiting for the other to declare something.

"You've changed how you're talking about the case," Henry finally said. "It used to be Logan v. Mississippi. Now it's… the system. Jim Crow. You make it sound like no one living ever made a choice."

Silas stopped pacing.

"I went to Alabama," he said.

Henry looked up. His expression didn't move, but something beneath it shifted, muscle tightening behind bone.

"Alabama?" Henry repeated. "What are you going to hear in Alabama that you wouldn't hear in Mississippi?

Silas sat, though he didn't fully relax into the chair. "I went because I heard about a man building an integrated studio there. Music made across color lines. I needed to see how someone did it – without being consumed."

Henry's voice was quiet. "And he told you how to try our case?"

Silas hesitated. "He gave me language for something I already sensed. That people defend what they think is theirs. If Mississippi believes I am attacking her, she will never listen. If I indict the system instead, she might."

Henry turned toward the window. A truck passed outside, and only when it faded did he speak.

"So, the wisdom we needed," he said sternly, "came from an Alabama White man. Not from the folks who've been living Jim Crow every hour of their lives. Not from my father or my mother. Not from the Negro teachers who get paid half what they're worth. Not from Greenville soil or Jackson pews or Farish Street men who learned to smile with their teeth shut."

Silas absorbed that like a blow he believed he deserved.

"I didn't go looking to replace what you know," he said. "I went because I realized I don't know enough."

Henry's jaw flexed. "It ain't the learning I mind. It's the burden. When you speak now – when you say 'system' instead of 'Mississippi' – I hear where the idea came from. And I wonder if that makes it cleaner for them, and harder for us."

Silas leaned forward. "You think I'm giving them an exit."

"I think," Henry said carefully, "that if the courtroom becomes a place where nobody is to blame, then nobody will answer. And I still have to live here when the papers are filed, and the lawyers go back to wherever they go."

Silas didn't respond immediately. He let the truth stand.

"It stings," Henry added, voice barely above breath, "because where we come from has taken so much. And now, the first help that might change anything... comes from the same direction that took."

Silas bowed his head, not in shame, but in comprehension. "Tell me what you need me to do."

Henry placed his hat on the chair beside him, smoothing the felt twice before he spoke.

"I need you to use whatever language wins," he said. "But I also need you to remember that some languages cost more than others. And when it's over – whether we win or lose – you're not the one going home alone through the same streets, unchanged."

Silas exhaled slowly. "I won't forget."

Henry stood – not abruptly, but with the care of someone preparing to walk back into a world that had never once permitted him.

"You better not," he said. Then, softer, almost swallowed by the room, "Because I didn't ask you to make this easier. I asked you to make it matter."

He left before Silas could answer, the door clicking shut like a gavel.

Silas looked down at that page on his desk. The caption was still correct. He checked it again for reassurance. After Henry's reaction, he didn't want to take any unnecessary chances.

LOGAN v. MISSISSIPPI
United States Southern District Court
Jackson Division

He let the page sit flat on the desk before him, smoothing over it with his palm. The office was quiet in the way courthouses never were – no echoing footsteps, no voices moving with purpose, only the hum of the fluorescent light above him and the ticking of the clock he had never bothered to set correctly. It ran five minutes fast. He preferred it that way because it reminded him that time took sides.

He had drafted and redrafted the opening section three times already, each version technically sound, each one rejected for reasons that had nothing to do with law.

The problem was not what he was alleging.

The problem was who would hear it.

Mississippi would hear it.

Not as a legal entity, that abstraction came later, but as a place. As memory. Their heritage. As something people loved without having to explain why. Silas understood that instinct. He shared it, though he rarely admitted as much even to himself. He had been raised inside its rules the way a child is raised inside a language: fluent long before conscious.

He needed to turn that fluency into an asset.

He reread the sentence he had underlined in pencil:

"The State of Mississippi, acting through its officers, has knowingly deprived the plaintiff of rights guaranteed under the Constitution of the United States."

It was true. Every word of it. Supported and defensible.

He crossed it out because he knew it would end the conversation before it began.

Silas turned the page and began again, this time starting not with the State but with the conduct.

"The plaintiff challenges a system of enforcement that operates through custom, ordinance, and discretionary application, resulting in the routine deprivation of constitutional rights under color of law."

There was the shift in context.

No geography. No names of people or places. No identity to defend, only structure.

He didn't pretend this was an act of generosity. It was a strategy. He had learned, years earlier, that people would concede almost anything about a system if they believed it didn't implicate them. They would criticize mechanisms they operated daily, condemn practices they relied upon, so long as they were allowed to believe those practices were somehow detachable from themselves.

Mississippi could remain intact, for now.

Jim Crow would absorb the consequence.

He didn't write the phrase. Everyone in the room would know what he meant. That was the advantage of a thing so old it no longer required naming. The law had learned to describe it without ever admitting it existed.

He continued drafting.

By mid-morning, the clerk, Brenda, knocked once and entered without waiting for a response. She carried a thin stack of papers, her posture careful, as though approaching a man engaged in something fragile.

"They've confirmed the chambers conference," she said. "Tomorrow morning. Judge Mathewson wants counsel present only."

Looking up, Silas mouthed, "Thank you."

She lingered a moment, eyes drifting to the papers spread across his desk. "This is… a complicated case."

"Yes," he said. "It is."

She hesitated. "But it's not …" She stopped herself. Smiled, apologetic. "Well. It's not what people are saying it is."

Silas looked up at her then. "What are people saying it is?"

"An attack."

"On what?"

Brenda considered, then shrugged. "On us, I suppose."

Silas let the silence answer for him. When she left, he didn't return to his drafting right away. Instead, he stood and walked to the window. From there, he could see the square – orderly, clean, almost geometric in its symmetry. Men moved through it with purpose. Others didn't linger long.

The square always had rules, even if he hadn't noticed them earlier.

He returned to his desk and added a marginal note in the draft, written lightly, almost to himself:

This case does not allege hatred. It alleges design.

At the Logans' house, there was a quiet that only rural nighttime could produce – no traffic, no neighbors, no sound except the faint hum of the refrigerator and the occasional creak of old boards settling.

Henry sat at the kitchen table, undershirt clinging to his back, boots still on though he had meant to take them off when he came in. A half-finished glass of water stood beside him. He had not taken a sip in over an hour.

Helen tied her robe as she walked into the room, her hair loose around her shoulders in a way no one outside the family ever saw. She knew better than to ask what was wrong. She had learned long ago that men like Henry, soft-spoken, raised to endure, will speak only after silence has worn down their defenses.

"You're still dressed," she said quietly, pulling out the chair across from him.

"I didn't feel like changing."

She waited.

Henry rubbed his thumb over the rim of the glass, circling it again and again like a man tracing the edge of something sharp.

"He went to Alabama," Henry finally said.

Helen's brows tightened, not sure where the sentence was headed. "Silas?"

"Yeah, he came back talking different. Speaking like he found something we've been too foolish to notice. Like the answers were sitting across the state line waiting for a man with a law degree."

Helen's exhale was slow. "Did he say that?"

"He didn't have to."

Another silence – this one heavier.

Henry was in his chair, its legs creaking. His voice lowered, almost to a confession.

"You know what it felt like? Like everything we've lived – every humiliation, every funeral, every man who never came home after being pulled from a truck or a jail cell – none of that was wisdom. Just... suffering. Useless. Like our pain is a story, not a lesson."

Helen rested her hands on the table, maintaining a calm and unwavering look.

"Silas is learning," she said. "And learning makes a man clumsy."

Henry shook his head. "I don't mind him learning. I mind that what changed him wasn't us. Wasn't me. Wasn't any Black soul who knows what it is to walk into a courtroom already sentenced."

Helen let the words sit. She knew better than to smooth them away.

"What did you tell him?" she asked.

"That I need him to make it matter, not easier." He stared down at his hands. "What I didn't say is – I want him to hurt a little. Not like us. But enough to know he's carrying something real. Enough that he wakes up with it. Enough that he loses sleep like I do."

"You want him to feel the cost."

Henry absorbed his own words. "Because if he doesn't feel it, I'm afraid he'll lay it down when it gets heavy. And I can't. I'll still be here."

Helen stood, walked around the table, and placed a hand on his shoulder. Not to comfort – comfort was too soft a word – to bear witness.

"You think he doesn't understand that?" she said.

"I think he understands it in his mind," Henry answered. "But he hasn't tasted it yet. Not in his mouth. Not in his bones. Not the way we have to."

Helen looked toward the window – the darkness beyond, the land that had shaped them both.

"You don't need him to be you," she said. "You need him to choose you. That's harder, and rarer."

Henry bowed his head.

"I hope he can."

Helen squeezed his shoulder again, firm and final.

"You hope. I will pray."

NINETEEN
Mississippi v. Jim Crow

Judge Mathewson listened without expression, his hands folded atop the file as though the case were already closed.

The court reporter waited, pen poised.

Paul Jenkins, the State's attorney, spoke first. He did so confidently, even generously, framing the matter as one of misunderstanding rather than malice. He spoke of local ordinances, of public safety, of discretion properly exercised. He never raised his voice.

"This court is not being asked to correct a wrong," Jenkins concluded. "It is being asked to indict a way of life."

Silas didn't object. He let the phrase hover in the room, knowing its usefulness depended on silence.

When it was his turn, he rose slowly, not for emphasis but control. He didn't begin with Henry Logan. He didn't begin with Mississippi. He began where courts felt safest – procedure.

"Your Honor," he said, "this case does not concern intent. It concerns effect."

Judge Mathewson's eyes narrowed slightly, clearly calculating.

"No one here is accused of animus," Silas continued. "No one is accused of cruelty. The plaintiff does not allege hatred. He alleges inevitability."

The word lingered, awkward in the room.

"What is at issue," Silas said, "is a structure that produces the same result regardless of who operates it. A structure that functions precisely as designed while permitting every individual within it to claim good faith."

Jenkins shifted, first crossing one leg, then the other. This was not the argument he had prepared to defeat. It was not an assault. It was an audit.

Silas leaned into that misalignment.

"The ordinances at issue do not name race," he said. "They rely instead on discretion, on timing, on enforcement after dark. Each component is defensible in isolation. Together, they form a regime."

He didn't use the forbidden phrase, though all three men felt its gravity.

Judge Mathewson interjected, his tone measured. "Mr. Thorn, are you asking this court to rule on the morality of local law?"

"No, Your Honor," Silas replied. "I am asking the court to examine its mechanics."

The answer appealed to the judge. Mechanics were impersonal. Mechanics allowed distance.

Silas felt the room loosen – not toward truth, but toward safety. The defendants no longer felt accused. The State no longer felt named. The system, abstracted from loyalty, stood exposed where it could be inspected without shame.

He allowed himself one final turn to mark its outline for the record that would follow.

"Your Honor," he said, "the State has asked, implicitly and explicitly, that this court preserve its dignity. That whatever is decided here not humiliate Mississippi before its citizens."

Jenkins' chin lifted slightly, unsure whether to claim or deny the premise.

Silas continued.

"Dignity is not something conferred at the end of a proceeding. It is not a courtesy extended once the record closes. Dignity is not what remains after harm is proven and responsibility is avoided."

His voice cooled rather than sharpened.

"If Mississippi believes it is entitled to dignity without first accounting for what has been done in its name – without acknowledging the systems it built, enforced, and defended – then this court is not being asked to preserve dignity."

He didn't raise his voice, and he didn't look away.

"It is being asked to protect the illusion of it. This case does not require this court to condemn Mississippi," Silas said.

"It requires the court to decide whether a legal structure that consistently deprives one class of citizens of constitutional protections can be insulated by its own familiarity," then he sat down.

Judge Mathewson said nothing. He closed the file in deferral.

Later, alone in his office, Silas reread the transcript. He knew he had succeeded strategically. He also knew what he had delayed.

By refusing to name Mississippi, he had allowed Mississippi to listen. But listening was not the same as accountability.

He placed the transcript into the file. On the inside cover, where no one else would see it, he wrote, not for the court, not for the record – to resist his own convenience:

Systems do not float above the soil that produces them.

He closed the file.

LOGAN v. MISSISSIPPI stared back at him, unchanged.

The law, at least, would not pretend otherwise.

***

Silas had not expected to return to the courthouse that afternoon. He was halfway down the marble steps when a voice called his name.

"Mr. Thorn?"

He turned.

A young woman stood inside the doorway. She wore a courthouse badge on a thin chain, the kind that suggested accommodation rather than authority. Her expression was stoic, so much so that only someone trained to read jurors would have noticed the urgency beneath it.

"I think this is yours," she said.

She held out a manila envelope. No address and no seal.

Silas didn't take it at once.

"I didn't leave anything inside," he said.

"I know," she replied.

Her voice lowered, barely enough to mark intention.

"Please don't say where you got it."

He accepted the envelope. She released it quickly, as though possession itself had already cost her.

Before the door closed, she added, "Some people think this place can't change. I don't know if that's true. But I know it won't if no one says anything."

The door shut.

***

Silas waited until he was inside his car – unsure if surveillance or clarity were his adversaries.

The memo was still warm from the copier. The first line tightened his jaw.

He read it once. Then again.

The courthouse columns rose ahead of him, intended to signal permanence. From this distance, permanence looked like neglect in formal wear.

The memo confirmed what he had sensed: the State was not afraid of losing. It was afraid of exposure.

Someone inside wanted him to know that.

Silas folded the memo carefully and placed it back inside the envelope. This would not go to Henry yet – not until he understood how the system would try to use his restraint against him.

He started the engine after a brief pause, and the day continued.

INTERNAL MEMORANDUM
Office of Legal Coordination – Jackson
CONFIDENTIAL – NOT FOR DISTRIBUTION

Re: *Post-Hearing Assessment – Logan v. Mississippi*

Summary:

Yesterday's chambers discussion didn't result in an adverse ruling, injunction, or formal finding. Counsel for Plaintiff adopted a procedural framing that avoided explicit allegations of racial animus or State intent. This approach reduced immediate institutional exposure and limited reputational risk.

Nuremberg, Mississippi

Observations:

1. Plaintiff's counsel appears committed to a systems-based theory of liability rather than adversarial personalization. This posture is strategically non-provocative and may attract academic or appellate interest without galvanizing public opposition.

2. Judicial receptivity increases when discussion remains focused on mechanics, process, and procedural application rather than historical grievance or moral critique.

3. There is no indication at present that the court seeks to embarrass or compel the State. Preservation of dignity remains achievable if escalation is avoided.

Risk Assessment:

While the legal theory itself is abstract, downstream consequences may arise if enforcement patterns are publicly aggregated. Exposure risk increases not through this courtroom, but through collateral attention – press, advocacy organizations, or federal review.

Recommended Actions:

- Maintain professional cooperation with Plaintiff's counsel to reinforce the tone of mutual respect.
- Avoid overt resistance that could be construed as retaliatory or defensive.
- Allow local enforcement discretion to continue operating within customary bounds, ensuring no deviations that could be mischaracterized as response-driven.
- Monitor Plaintiff's personal circumstances only insofar as necessary to anticipate external narrative shifts.

Conclusion:

The hearing reflects a manageable trajectory. The case is not currently dangerous.

Its danger lies in what others may choose to make of it.

Nuremberg, Mississippi

TWENTY
Mrs. Logan

S ilas dialed three times before letting it ring through. Each time, he'd hung up after the first ring, rehearsing what he would say.

When Helen finally answered, her "Yes?" carried the weight of someone who had been expecting this call and dreading it.

"Mrs. Logan, I wonder if...." He stopped. Started over.

"Would you be willing to meet me for lunch?"

The pause lasted long enough for him to hear his own breathing.

"We can do that," she said.

He asked if Henry and Helen would be willing to meet him for lunch in Corinth – middle ground, close enough to be practical, far enough to feel impersonal. He didn't explain why or explain what had changed. He simply said he thought it would be useful to talk.

Helen answered. Her voice was steady, familiar in its courtesy.

"Yes," she said after a brief pause. "We can do that."

She didn't qualify the answer. She didn't mention Henry's schedule.

Silas arrived early. He parked across the street from the diner and sat in his car, reviewing nothing. The building was modest – brick, a single plate-glass window, a door that closed too slowly. He watched people come and go with the practiced distance of someone who had spent his career observing rooms before entering them.

When Helen's car pulled in, he reached for his briefcase.

The action was conscious. He could have left it behind. Nothing inside it would be needed. But he brought it anyway, snapping it shut before stepping out of the car, as if the sound itself might establish terms. To anyone watching, the message would be unambiguous: this was business, or at least something that insisted on resembling it.

Helen saw the briefcase. She noted it without saying anything.

Inside, the diner smelled like Southern home cooking. They took a booth near the window. Silas placed the briefcase beside him, upright, close enough to touch, but he didn't open it.

They ordered. Polite phrases passed between them – weather, traffic, the drive. It was not until the waitress walked away that Helen spoke plainly.

"Henry won't be coming," she said.

Silas looked at her, then instinctively toward the door, as though Henry might arrive late.

"I thought ..." he began.

"He had to go to Jackson this morning," Helen said. "Work that couldn't wait. I didn't think it necessary to cancel with you."

Silas nodded. The nod came too quickly, the reflex of someone accustomed to adjusting plans without examining the reason.

"Of course," he said. "That's fine."

It was not fine. He understood that but didn't say so.

They sat in a brief, careful silence. Helen folded her hands on the table. Silas rested one hand on the briefcase, not gripping it, but keeping it present.

"I appreciate you coming," he said. "I didn't want to presume."

"You didn't," Helen replied. "You asked."

There was no gratitude in her tone. It was the voice of someone accustomed to clarifying facts before allowing conclusions.

Silas took a breath.

"I've been reviewing the file again," he said. "Some details I – some things I hadn't fully accounted for."

Helen watched him closely now, assessing.

"You've been reading," she said.

"Yes."

"And listening?" she asked.

The question was not framed as an accusation, but it carried a deeper meaning.

"I'm trying to," Silas said.

She acknowledged his sincerity.

"All right," she said. "Then I'll tell you some things Henry won't."

She didn't begin with the arrest, or the charge, or the night itself. She began with mornings. "There are days he can't get out of bed without help," she said. "He doesn't like that anyone knows."

"Is this related to ..."

"One doctor called it a rheumatism," Helen said. "Another said it might be nerve-related. The county physician wrote *chronic inflammatory episodes* and left it at that. They prescribed rest when he could afford it, aspirin when he couldn't."

She stopped for a moment.

"Stress makes it worse. So does standing too long. So does being told to keep going like pain was a character flaw."

Silas listened without interruption.

"He doesn't talk about it," she continued. "He's not ashamed of it. He doesn't believe it should matter."

Silas glanced down at the briefcase, then back to her.

"But it does," he said.

"Yes," Helen replied. "It does."

She sipped her sweet tea.

"He missed work last week," she said. "That's not like him. He told his supervisor it was a stomach bug. It wasn't. It was pain that made it difficult to stand for more than a few minutes at a time."

Silas felt the word *timing* surface in his mind, unwanted but persistent.

"This condition," he said carefully. "Has it been documented?"

Helen's mouth tightened.

"Everything about Henry is documented," she said. "Just not in places that help him."

Their food arrived. Neither of them touched it immediately.

"I want to understand him better," Silas said. "Not the case. Him."

Helen made direct eye contact with him.

"Then you need to understand this," she said. "Henry does not believe the law is designed to recognize people like him when they are vulnerable. He believes it notices them only when they are upright enough to be punished."

Silas didn't respond.

"He didn't want me to come today," she added. "He worries that once you know too much, you'll start thinking in terms of risk instead of justice."

Silas felt the sentence hit hard.

"And will I?" he asked.

"That depends," she said, "on whether you think vulnerability is an argument or an inconvenience."

The briefcase remained closed between them.

When they stood to leave, Silas carried it out again, as deliberately as he had carried it in. Outside, he paused beside Helen's car.

"Thank you," he said. The words felt insufficient, but he didn't reach for better ones.

"Henry will ask what we talked about," she said. "I'll tell him the truth."

"And what is that?" Silas asked.

"That you're beginning to see him," she said. "Not as a case, and not as a symbol."

She unlocked her car and opened the door.

"As a man who is already paying more than the record will ever show," as she drove away.

Silas remained standing for a moment longer, the briefcase heavy at his side, less protective now than it had been when he arrived.

He understood, uncomfortably, that it no longer functioned as a barrier at all.

She and Henry arrived home at nearly the same time. As she filled him in on the lunch with Silas, Henry didn't interrupt her.

They were in the kitchen. Evening light pressed thinly through the window above the sink. Helen stood with her back to the counter, and Henry sat at the table, his hands flat on the wood, grounding himself.

"He brought his briefcase," Helen said. "Didn't open it once."

Henry recognized that pattern.

"You told him," he said.

"Yes."

"Everything?"

"Enough."

He audibly exhaled.

"I didn't want him thinking …"

"I know," Helen said. "You didn't want him thinking in terms of mercy."

Henry shifted in his chair. The movement cost him more than he let on.

"Mercy expires," he said. "Justice is supposed to hold."

Helen crossed the room and rested a hand on the back of his chair, not touching him directly.

"He asked whether vulnerability was an argument or an inconvenience," she said.

Henry looked up at that.

"And what did you tell him?"

"That it depends on the man asking."

Henry considered this.

"He won't say it out loud," he said. "But now he knows the cost."

"That was the point," Helen replied.

"Next time," he said quietly, "I'll go with you."

Helen didn't contradict him.

TWENTY-ONE
The Cost of Abstraction

The first consequence didn't arrive as retaliation.

It arrived as relief.

Silas heard it in the voices before he recognized it in himself.

The phone rang at 8:10 p.m. A colleague from Jackson — someone who had stopped returning his calls months earlier — spoke warmly, even admiringly.

"You threaded the needle yesterday," the man said. "That's not easy in a room like that."

Silas thanked him, reflexively.

Another call followed. Then another.

One man praised the restraint. Another praised the tone. A third praised the fact that no one had been embarrassed.

By mid-morning, Silas had heard the same word four or five times.

Measured.

It was said as a compliment. It sounded like absolution.

At the courthouse, clerks who had grown distant now looked him in his eyes again. One offered coffee. Another lingered at his doorway, asking – casually – how long he thought the case might take.

The case had not changed.

The way it was being received had.

At lunch, Silas sat alone in a café he used to frequent with other attorneys. Today, two men he knew noticed him from another table but didn't invite him over. One raised his cup in a small salute, as though Silas had crossed a line they approved of without requiring them to follow.

The newspaper arrived mid-afternoon. The article was short and careful. Buried beneath zoning disputes and other municipal news.

Federal Hearing Questions Ordinance Enforcement Practices

No plaintiff named.
No defendant identified.
No language sharp enough to bruise.
Mississippi appeared only as a setting.

Silas folded the paper and placed it in his briefcase. He didn't feel victorious. He felt something worse. He felt welcomed back.

Across town, Henry felt none of it.

He stood outside the lumber yard after 1 o'clock, toolbox resting at his feet and eyes fixed straight ahead. Two men leaned against a truck nearby, talking loudly enough to be heard.

A foreman emerged, clipboard tucked beneath his arm. He scanned the yard, then turned away.

Henry waited the length of time that could still be described as reasonable.

Then he picked up his tools and left.

At the feed store, the clerk avoided his eyes.

"We're out," the man said, gesturing vaguely toward the back.

Henry had learned long ago that protest was useless.

Outside, the sun beat down with a Southern brutality. Henry adjusted his hat and walked the long way home because it delayed the explanation he would owe.

When Silas arrived at the Logan house that evening, the porch light was already on.

Helen opened the door.

"They liked your argument," she said.

Silas hesitated, unsure if it was praise or a warning.

Henry sat at the kitchen table, the Green Book open beside him but untouched. The pages had not been turned.

"You didn't name them," Henry said.

"No," Silas replied.

"And they noticed."

Silas pulled out the folded newspaper and placed it on the table. Helen read the headline.

"They're listening," Silas said.

Henry lifted his eyes, maintaining a calm and deliberate stare. "They always listen when they don't feel accused."

Helen spoke quietly. "And while they listen, they tighten everything else."

Silas exhaled. "That's why the next step matters."

"Make sure the distance you're buying them doesn't become the distance they bury us in."

Silas didn't answer right away. He could not promise something he had not yet learned how to control.

Later that night, a patrol car slowed at the corner.

Not enough to stop, and not enough to justify complaint, but enough to be seen.

Helen watched from the window.

"They didn't do that yesterday," she said.

"No," Henry replied. "Yesterday they were deciding."

In Jackson, Silas reread the memo from the envelope:

The meeting concluded without a vote.

No formal recommendation was necessary, as the stated purpose was purely informational.

After everyone else had departed, three men remained. Coffee cooled in paper cups nearby, and a window had been left slightly open, allowing the sounds of traffic below to drift intermittently into the room.

"The issue," one of them stated, "is not about legality. We've confirmed that time and again."

No one disagreed.

"What we're observing," another added, tapping the edge of the file, "is consistency. And whether people appreciate it or not, consistency stabilizes expectations."

Silence followed. The file remained unopened.

"If we intervene," the first man continued, "we introduce variance. Exceptions. That invites scrutiny."

"From who?" someone inquired.

"Everyone," he answered. "Including those we prefer not to question us."

There was a fleeting moment when the conversation could have taken a different turn, but it didn't.

"The patterns are clear," the second man remarked. "Predictable. That's important."

"And what about the individual?" the third asked, genuinely.

The first man simply shrugged. "Individuals resolve themselves. It's the systems that endure."

That concluded the discussion.

The file was marked and added to the others.

No action recommended at this time.

The language was cautious, professional, and predictive.

Risk increases if narrative personalization resumes. Recommend continued emphasis on systemic review.

It allowed them to say they are listening while adjusting pressure elsewhere – where no transcript existed.

He closed the file.

For the first time, he felt the burden of what Henry had already been carrying: that survival often depended not on winning arguments, but on enduring their consequences.

Abstraction had opened the door. But someone would have to stand in it.

And Silas was beginning to understand that while the law allowed him to step back, Henry never could.

He sat at his desk and pulled the Logan file from his briefcase, but he didn't open it.

Instead, he took out a blank legal pad and wrote at the top:

What I Didn't See

Then he wrote:

I thought restraint was protection.

I thought if I kept the argument narrow enough, clinical enough, the harm would stay manageable.

I thought Henry understood that I was helping him survive.

He stopped, set the pen down, then picked it up again.

But survival and dignity aren't the same thing.

Last week, a woman with a red ribbon asked me to dance. And I hesitated, because some part of me was calculating whether it was safe. Whether someone might see. Whether crossing that line would cost me something I couldn't afford to lose.

And Henry watched me hesitate.

He watched me do the math.

That math – that constant calculation of safety – is what I've been asking him to accept as victory. As progress. As the best the law can offer.

But he doesn't get to stop calculating when the hearing ends.

I do.

He pressed his palms flat against the desk.

I told myself I was being strategic. That moderation was wisdom. That by refusing to name Mississippi directly, I was giving the court room to listen.

But what I gave the court was an exit.

And what I gave Henry was exposure.

The system heard my careful language and learned it could continue, just more quietly.

Silas looked up at the window. The square would wake soon.

In a couple of days, court will resume, and the case will proceed on the terms that I had set. Henry knew this before I did.

That's why he asked me to take the case. Not because he thought I could win. Because he needed someone who would stay.

Stay through the retaliation, through the delays, even when reason said to withdraw.

He needed a witness with credentials.

And I thought he needed a lawyer.

The realization didn't arrive as guilt. It arrived as clarity that made guilt seem too self-focused.

I cannot give him back what this case has already cost.

I cannot make the system fair by arguing more carefully.

What I can do – what I have to do – is stop pretending that my discomfort and his danger are equivalent.

Stop pretending that naming the machinery and dismantling it are the same thing.

Stop pretending that the law's patience is a virtue when someone else pays for the wait.

He tore the page from the pad, folded it, and placed it in the inside pocket of his jacket.

Not to forget, and not to forgive himself.

To remember, when the case proceeded, when the consequences arrived, when the outcome disappointed, exactly whose choice had made it possible.

Melvin E. Edwards

TWENTY-ONE AND ONE-HALF
Policy

Caroline's breathing changed first, though not dramatically. It was a thinning, a faint whistle that appeared between her ribs like a thread being pulled too tight.

Helen noticed it while folding towels.

Caroline sat on the living room rug with her crayons, careful with her hands, and tired in a way children shouldn't be.

Helen watched for three breaths. Then three more.

"Baby," she said gently, "come here."

Caroline stood and walked over slowly.

Helen put her palm against the child's chest.

The rhythm was wrong.

"Daniel," Helen said, voice level, "go get your daddy."

Daniel ran down the hall.

Helen crossed into the kitchen and opened the cabinet above the sink where she kept what mattered: bandages, aspirin, a thermometer, and the inhaler.

It wasn't there.

She checked again, slower this time, her hand moving through the shelf with the calm of someone refusing to admit panic to herself.

Then she remembered. It was in her purse. Because she had been rationing it.

She retrieved it, shook it once, and felt the truth in the sound.

Something serious was wrong.

Henry appeared in the doorway.

"What is it?" he asked.

Helen did not look up. "Caroline's tight."

Henry moved closer to assess the situation for himself.

Helen crouched beside Caroline, and Henry stood beside Helen.

"Open your mouth," she said.

Caroline obeyed.

Helen gave one puff, then waited. It helped, but only slightly.

"She needs a refill," Helen said.

Henry glanced at the clock. The pharmacy closed at five and he didn't have much time.

"I'll go," he said.

Helen's voice stayed steady. "Take cash."

Henry paused. "Why?"

Helen looked at him. "Because the account may not be there."

Henry checked his wallet. He didn't have enough.

Helen opened the bread box and took out the small envelope she never called savings. Mostly twenties – money she peeled away from groceries and other things when she could. She handed it to him.

At the pharmacy, the bell above the door chimed.

The clerk was a young woman Henry had seen before. She did not greet him by name today.

Her eyes went to the counter, not his face.

Henry slid the prescription card forward.

"My daughter needs this refilled," he said.

The clerk took it, turned, and pulled a file drawer open with the papers that had started to fray from frequent handling.

She thumbed through cards — the only record-keeping that looked official enough to become final. She returned with the card and did not hand it back.

She slid the drawer shut and opened a worn ledger on the counter, names in one column, dates in another, amounts written in tight pencil that had been retraced so many times it looked like ink.

She ran her finger down the page until it stopped at LOGAN, HENRY, then paused as if the paper itself had instructed her to be careful.

"It's marked," she said quietly. "I can't run you on the book today."

"What does that mean," Henry asked.

"Mr. Logan," she said, and the tone of it was much more administrative than friendly.

"Yes," Henry replied.

She spoke carefully, as if repeating something she had been trained to say.

"The charge account is on hold."

Henry stared at her.

"What do you mean on hold?" he asked.

The clerk's eyes flicked down to the card.

"Review," she said, as if the word were the final authority.

Henry kept his voice level. "We've had that account for years."

The clerk nodded without disagreeing or validating.

"It's not saying you did anything," she added, almost retreating. "Just says **cash only until it clears**."

Henry pulled out the envelope and counted bills slowly, because dignity required slowness when the world wanted you frantic.

The clerk took the cash and opened a metal drawer that rang softly when it slid.

Then she looked back at the card.

Her eyebrows lifted.

"What?" Henry asked.

The clerk's mouth tightened.

"I can't refill it without the doctor's say-so," she said.

Henry blinked. "It's an inhaler."

Her face was apologetic for half a second before tightening again into policy.

"Refill limit," she said. "He wrote it 'no refills' last time."

Henry leaned in slightly.

"My child can't breathe right," he said. It wasn't a threat. It was a serious fact.

The clerk swallowed.

"You'll have to get him to call it in," she said.

Henry asked, "Can you reach him?"

The clerk shook her head. "Office closes at four on Wednesdays."

Henry looked at the clock.

She turned the prescription card so he could see the doctor's handwriting – <u>NO REFILLS</u>, underlined, and a short signature at the bottom like a final stamp.

"He's the only one who can change it," she said. "Not me and not the register. If I break the book, I lose this job."

Henry glanced at the wall clock and felt the hour for what it was – after four, when the town's offices went quiet and the rules became harder to navigate.

"How long?" he asked.

The clerk hesitated.

"Tomorrow," she said. "If he's in."

Henry stared at the shelves behind her – rows of medicine waiting to be claimed.

Availability was not the problem. Access was.

"So, you have it," he said.

The clerk nodded.

"And you won't give it to me," he said.

Her face flushed.

"I can't," she said quickly. "Not without his instruction."

Henry froze for a second. He did not argue further, choosing to turn and leave.

At home, Helen met him at the door and read his face before he spoke.

"No?" she asked.

Henry shook his head.

"What did they say?" Helen asked.

"They said the account is on hold," Henry replied. "And the doctor wrote in 'no refills.'"

In the living room, Caroline's breathing had become audible — thin, whistling, like a kettle that would not pacify.

Helen lifted Caroline into her arms.

"Get the car," she said.

Henry went to the phone first.

It was a rotary phone on the kitchen wall. He dialed the doctor's office and listened to the ring travel nowhere.

No answer.

He called the hospital.

The operator answered and transferred him once, then again.

A nurse finally picked up.

Henry spoke slowly and carefully.

"My little girl needs her inhaler refilled," he said. "The pharmacy won't do it, and the doctor's office is closed."

The nurse asked questions in an order that did not honor his emergency: name, age, weight, symptoms.

Helen spoke from the doorway, controlled but sharp enough to cut through procedure.

"She can't finish a sentence," Helen said.

The nurse paused.

"Bring her in," she said.

Henry asked, "Can you send someone?"

The nurse hesitated, then answered as if reciting a rule.

"We don't have an ambulance to spare unless it's already dispatched," she said.

"Who dispatches it?" Henry asked.

"Sheriff," she said. "Or the town operator."

Henry hung up and dialed again.

"Operator," he said when the woman answered, "connect me to the sheriff's office."

The operator's voice cooled slightly. "What's the emergency?"

"My daughter can't breathe," Henry said.

A pause, then the line clicked and began to ring.

A deputy answered.

Henry gave the address.

The deputy asked, "Is she conscious?"

"Yes," Henry replied.

"Any bleeding?" the deputy asked.

"No."

When the deputy asked his name, there was a pause long enough to be noticed.

"We'll see what we can do," the deputy said.

Henry stared at the receiver.

"How long?" he asked.

The deputy answered carefully, as if time itself could become a promise he didn't want attached to his name.

"Depends on where the unit is," he said.

Henry hung up.

Helen was already at the door with Caroline.

They did not wait.

They drove.

The drive to the hospital took eleven minutes. Henry knew this because he had timed it before, on a day when nothing was wrong, during a period when knowing such things felt like preparation rather than necessity. It was a lesson he had learned from Helen. Tonight was the test, not the lesson.

Helen held Caroline in the back seat. The child's breathing had evened slightly, but the quality of it was still wrong – shallow in the way of a thing that had used up most of what it had. Helen kept one hand flat against her chest and counted without counting. She did not tell Henry what she was counting.

He drove at the speed that would not attract attention. He had learned long ago that there were two ways to be stopped on a Mississippi road at night, and the second was no better than the first.

Daniel sat in the front seat without being told. He already understood enough of the silence to know what his job was, which was to be useful without getting in the way.

The hospital entrance was lit from above. Henry pulled up to the main doors.

"Go," Helen said.

He went.

The woman at the desk was completing a form when he reached the counter. She did not look up immediately. When she did, her expression arranged itself into the practiced neutrality of someone who had learned to apply the same face to all circumstances.

"My daughter can't breathe right," Henry said. "She needs her inhaler refilled. The pharmacy wouldn't ..."

"Name?"

"Logan. Caroline Logan. She's four."

"What's the nature of the complaint?"

Henry looked at her. "She can't breathe."

The woman nodded, completing the form. She slid it across the counter. "Fill out what you can. Someone will be with you shortly."

He filled out the form at the counter rather than taking it to a seat, because taking it to a seat meant time, and time meant something different tonight than it usually did.

Helen arrived carrying Caroline. The child's breathing was audible now – not labored exactly, but requiring intentional effort. Helen held her against her shoulder and stood without moving toward a chair, as though sitting down were a concession she wasn't prepared to make.

Henry returned the form.

"Someone will be with you," the woman said again.

Helen found a chair in the corner near the window and sat. She kept Caroline upright against her chest, which was better. She had read this somewhere, or been told it, or simply learned it the way she had learned most things – by paying attention to what worked.

The waiting room was half full. A man across the room had a wrapped hand. Two women sat together near the door, speaking quietly. No one looked at the Logans, which was itself a form of looking.

Henry sat beside Helen. He folded his hands on his knees and looked at the floor between his feet. He was calculating. He had been calculating since the pharmacy, since the answer about the account, and since the dispatcher's pause on the phone.

He was calculating whether any part of this would have gone differently if his name had been something else. He arrived at the answer he always arrived at and did not say it aloud.

Caroline shifted against Helen's shoulder. "Mama," she said.

"I'm here," Helen said.

"Is it almost done?"

Helen pressed her lips against the top of Caroline's head. "Almost, Baby."

A nurse appeared in the doorway, clipboard in hand. She called a name, and a man rose and followed her through the door. The door closed.

Henry looked at the clock on the wall. It had been fourteen minutes since they arrived.

He stood and returned to the counter.

The woman looked up.

"She's four years old," Henry said. "She has asthma. Her regular medication ran out, and the pharmacy couldn't refill it. I need someone to look at her."

"Sir, someone will be with you as soon as …"

"She's been waiting fourteen minutes."

The woman's expression didn't change. "We're seeing patients in order of medical urgency."

Henry placed both hands on the counter, flat, so there could be no confusion about their position.

"My daughter cannot breathe," he said.

The word "cannot" carried the weight he intended. Not is having trouble. Not is uncomfortable. Cannot.

The woman held his gaze for a moment, then looked past him toward Helen and Caroline in the corner. Something in her expression shifted – not much, but enough.

"Let me see what I can do," she said.

He thanked her and returned to his seat. Helen had not watched the exchange. She had kept her eyes on Caroline, which was its own form of wisdom. What you don't see, you cannot react to. What you cannot react to cannot be used against you.

A different nurse appeared six minutes later. Young and efficient, she seemed like the kind of person who moved through a room like it belonged to her.

"Caroline Logan?"

Henry and Helen stood together.

The nurse led them through a door and down a short corridor, past rooms whose curtains were partly drawn. She directed them to a small bay near the end and asked Helen to set Caroline on the table. She listened to Caroline's breathing with a stethoscope, asked two questions, then left briefly and returned with a small nebulizer.

The treatment took twelve minutes. Caroline sat very still, as children sometimes do when they understand, without being told, that stillness is what is needed. The machine hummed. Her breathing changed in increments – slow at first, then more even, then fuller than it had been in hours.

Henry watched her. He did not look at his hands. He did not look at Helen. He watched his daughter breathe.

When the nurse returned to check the results, she confirmed that Caroline's oxygen levels had stabilized. She said the word stabilized in a tone that suggested resolution. Henry understood the word to mean something more temporary than that.

A physician came eventually. He was brief and professional. He wrote the prescription in less than a minute, tore it from the pad, and extended it toward Henry without looking at him.

"Fill this in the morning," the physician said. "Follow up with her regular doctor by the end of the week."

Henry took the prescription.

He didn't say what he was thinking, which was that her regular doctor had written no refills on the last prescription for reasons no one had explained. He didn't say that her regular doctor's office had closed at four and that no one had answered the phone. He didn't even say that the account at the pharmacy had been placed on hold two days after the filing of a federal lawsuit that bore his name.

He said, "Thank you."

The physician had already moved on.

In the car on the way home, Caroline fell asleep against Helen's arm before they reached the end of the hospital parking lot. Daniel rode in the front again. He had asked no questions the entire night. Henry had noticed this.

"She'll be all right," Henry said, though it was not quite a question.

"Yes," Helen said.

They drove in silence for a while. The road was empty. Henry kept his speed even.

"The prescription," Helen said.

"I have it."

He knew what she was thinking. In the morning, he would go to the pharmacy. He would pay cash. If cash was not enough, the prescription said what it said and could not be filled without the physician calling it in, and the physician was already three patients down the corridor by the time they left.

Henry thought: There will always be another step. That is the design of it.

He did not say this because Daniel was in the car and awake.

When they arrived home, Henry carried Caroline inside. She did not wake. He set her in her bed and stood for a moment in the doorway of her room, listening to her breathe. It was even and full. It was ordinary, which was all he had wanted.

Helen walked up beside him. She did not say anything. She stood where he stood.

After a while, Henry said, very quietly, "I keep thinking about that pause."

Helen waited.

"On the phone. When the deputy heard my name." He did not look at her. "It wasn't long, but it was there."

Helen said, "I know."

"If we had waited for the ambulance..." Henry said.

He didn't finish the sentence.

Helen took his hand. Not to comfort him, but to confirm something. That she had been in the same room and had heard the same pause. She also made sure he understood that no matter what, this cost would be paid by both of them together.

"Go to bed," she said.

"In a while," he said.

She left him there. He stayed until he was certain that what he was hearing was just breathing – ordinary and reliable breathing – and then he went to bed too, where he lay awake for a long time, watching the ceiling, calculating nothing in particular, which was its own kind of rest.

TWENTY-ONE AND THREE-FOURTHS
No Motion

Silas learned about it the way the town preferred such things be learned: indirectly. Thankfully, he now knew Caroline would recover after speaking to Henry and Helen a couple of days after the medical incident.

Then he started hearing the delayed chatter in the corridor outside the clerk's office while stepping aside to let two men pass.

"Logan's little girl," one man said.

The other replied, "I heard. Breathing problems. She's in the hospital because her old man couldn't pay for the medicine she needed."

A pause, then the phrase went uncorrected in a way that allowed a rumor to become colloquially factual.

"Just one of them things," the man added, plainly.

Silas stopped walking.

His hand remained on the courthouse railing to steady himself.

His mind immediately reached for sequence; for something he could name. A challenge. A file. Anything.

He returned to his office without speaking to anyone, then closed the door before sitting.

Then he did what he had trained himself to do when confronted with harm: he began to draft.

He pulled out a legal pad and wrote, in neat capital letters:

EMERGENCY PETITION

He underlined it twice.

Injunctive relief.

Order to compel.

Contempt.

Mandamus.

His hand moved quickly, assembling jurisdiction and standards notes the way it always did – irreparable harm, likelihood of success, and balance of equities.

And then his momentum slowed, because none of it fit.

Caroline Logan was not a party. This was not a docket entry, and there was no right that the county had denied her on paper.

No ordinance on the book prohibited medicine.

No deputy confiscated an inhaler.

No clerk wrote "denied" in ink.

The town had done what it always did: distributed the harm across enough offices that each person could claim they had only followed routine.

Silas stared at the words on the page.

EMERGENCY PETITION

He realized, with cold clarity, that the emergency had already happened.

And that the law — the law he had trusted as corrective mechanism — had no instrument for what was most real.

He tore the page out, then folded it until it fit in his pocket. Not because it would be filed, but because he needed to feel he still possessed a contemporaneous record.

Outside his window, the square moved in its ordinary time. Men walked, cars passed, and the courthouse remained lit.

Silas sat alone and understood the shape of the system's genius: It could kill without ever issuing an order to do so.

He put his pen down.

For the first time since agreeing to represent Henry Logan, Silas felt the law not as a tool — but as a limit.

And the limit did not bend.

Nuremberg, Mississippi

TWENTY-TWO
The Reasoning

The transcript stood alone, and Silas knew if he read it again, it wouldn't lead to a different outcome.

Instead, he sat at his desk after midnight, the courthouse long emptied of its daily theater, the building reduced to what it truly was: corridors, paper, and light left on for no one in particular. The file lay open but untouched. He had learned, recently, that proximity to documents didn't require engagement. Sometimes the greater act was refusing to pretend they were procedural.

The hearing replayed itself anyway.

Judge Mathewson's careful questions.

The State's attorney's visible relief when the word Mississippi went unspoken.

The way the room had leaned toward abstraction the moment it was offered permission.

Silas understood now what he had done.

He had made it easier to listen.

And by doing so, he had made it easier not to answer.

Courts preferred systems over people because systems could be examined without demanding repentance. You could study a mechanism endlessly without ever asking who had built it, who had maintained it, or who had benefited from its consistency.

Silas rested his forearms on the desk and stared at the margin where he had written his reminder:

Systems do not float above the soil that produces them.

It was true. And it was insufficient.

Because systems didn't enforce themselves. They were animated – quietly, dutifully – by people who believed compliance absolved them of authorship.

This was not about scale or visibility; it was about logic – the same administrative reasoning that had once made Nuremberg possible without requiring most of its participants to believe themselves cruel.

The recognition was not revolutionary.

Silas didn't recoil from it, or rush to qualify it. He understood the danger of reflexive defense, of insisting difference before acknowledging similarity of method. He had spent his professional life watching men survive moral inquiry by insisting they had followed rules rather than exercised judgment.

What bothered him was not the comparison.

It was the trains that kept running on time.

He had argued that the court need not condemn Mississippi. That it could examine mechanics without naming hands, and that the structure itself was the injury.

And the court had listened.

That was the problem.

Listening didn't disturb power. Listening refined it.

Silas leaned back and closed his eyes. He thought of Henry – of how abstraction landed on someone who didn't have the luxury of existing as an idea. Of how language that felt clean in court could translate into delay, exposure, or reprisal once it crossed into life.

Silence, he realized, had never been procedural. But abstraction could be lethal in ways silence never was.

Silence at least acknowledged presence. Abstraction erased it.

He opened the file again, not to revise the caption, but to read the facts as they would be lived. Arrest times. Ordinance numbers. Enforcement patterns that repeated with such regularity they could be mistaken for scripts.

Henry's life appeared there only as data.

That, too, was someone else's choice.

Silas reached for a pen and wrote beneath his earlier note, slower this time, pressing hard enough to leave an imprint on the page below:

If no one is named, someone will still pay.

He capped the pen and closed the file.

The case would proceed.

The strategy would hold – for now.

But Silas understood something he had not allowed himself to articulate before:

If justice arrived without attribution, it would arrive incomplete. And if it arrived incomplete, it would ask the already-burdened to carry the remainder.

Outside, the clock in the square struck three times.

Silas turned off the lamp and stood in the dark, no longer certain that illumination was always an ethical good. Some truths, he was learning, demanded not exposure, but ownership.

And ownership, once claimed, could not be set down.

TWENTY-THREE
Henry, Not Hank

Bullock's office was narrow and bright, with files stacked where clients could see them. The desk held a legal pad and a cold mug; everything else had been put away.

Bullock closed the door himself and gestured to the chair.

"I'll be brief," he said. "You're busy."

"Am I?" Silas said.

"A case like yours gets noticed," Bullock said. "Most of it stays polite. Some of it doesn't."

"People are wondering what you think you're doing," Bullock said.

Silas didn't answer.

"Things circulate," Bullock added. "Not always through channels." He looked at Silas, checking how the sentence had been interpreted. "They think you're pulling on a thread."

"Meaning?" Silas said.

Bullock's mouth moved as if he might choose a longer explanation, then didn't.

"You're asking them to say out loud what they usually leave unsaid. Intentions are safe. Effects are not."

"I'm asking for a record."

Bullock glanced at the notepad before looking away, as though setting that part of the discussion aside where it fit best.

"Separate problem… my house. I've taken on too many new clients. There's a leak under the sink. My wife's stopped mentioning it, which is worse."

"Plumbing?"

"And whatever comes after it fails," Bullock said.

"I might know someone," Silas said.

Bullock's expression shifted. "Not you?"

"Him," Silas said. "Henry Logan. He's careful."

Bullock held the name a moment. "Your client."

"Yes."

"Send him."

Silas stood, and Bullock met him at the door and offered his hand.

"Be careful," Bullock said.

Silas shook his hand. "I will."

Henry arrived the following Saturday.

The yard was freshly cut and otherwise left alone. Henry parked along the curb, removed his hat, and knocked.

Bullock answered the door himself.

"You're Hank, right?"

"Henry."

Bullock nodded.

Under the sink, a slow drip darkened the cabinet floor. Henry crouched, ran his hand along the pipe, and tightened a fitting without saying a word. He tested it, watched, then wiped his hands on a cloth. Then he started in on repairing the damaged woodwork.

Bullock stood against the counter. "Silas speaks well of you."

"He's been fair," Henry said.

Bullock's eyes stayed on him. "That's an interesting word."

Henry folded the cloth and stuffed it into his back pocket. "It's the right one."

Bullock watched him pack his things.

"Your name comes up," Bullock said.

Henry didn't look surprised. "I don't doubt it."

"Not always kindly," Bullock said.

"I can't control that."

"No," Bullock said. "You can't."

As Henry moved toward the door, Bullock said, almost as an afterthought, "If you ever need a call returned, tell Silas to tell me."

Henry stopped. He turned back enough to look Bullock in the eye.

"I appreciate that," Henry said.

Outside, the sunlight was relentless. Henry put his hat back on, got into the truck, and drove away.

Bullock stood in the doorway until the truck turned the corner.

PART V: JUDGMENT

TWENTY-FOUR
Course Correction

Silas didn't say Mississippi. He didn't say county, clerk, or judge. He didn't say the state. He spoke instead in shapes and sequences, in the exclusive understanding of a way of life.

He described how discretion functioned. How authority was rarely exercised in grand declarations, but in intervals – moments where nothing happened, where no record was made, where the absence of action carried more force than any ruling.

He spoke of predictability. Of systems that congratulated themselves on nondiscrimination because their outcomes appeared consistent.

The judge listened intently.

Jenkins nodded.

Silas moved carefully, as though stepping across ice whose thickness he hadn't tested in advance. He framed each sentence so that agreement was not only possible, but unavoidable. When he spoke of local customs, Jenkins murmured assent. When he spoke of judicial economy, of order, of minimizing disruption, the State's attorney actually smiled.

It was the strangest alignment Silas had ever felt — this sense that his argument was being welcomed because it was misunderstood. Or worse, because it was understood and approved.

"Stability," Silas said, "is not maintained by proclamation. It is maintained by repetition."

Jenkins made a note.

Silas continued. "What concerns this court is not hostility. It is habit."

Jenkins glanced at the judge, then back at Silas, nodding again.

Silas felt the room relax. The gallery was quiet in the way of rooms that believe they know where they are headed.

That was when he saw Henry.

Not at first. At first, it was a movement out of the corner of his eye — a shift that didn't belong to the rhythm of the room. Henry had straightened in his chair. His hands were clenched, then released, then clenched again. He stretched his fingers as though trying to pull sensation back into them.

Silas stopped speaking in the middle of his sentence.

Henry's jaw was tight. His eyes were fixed forward and his forehead was sweaty. He rolled his shoulders slightly, then winced, enough that Silas could clearly see it.

Helen's words returned to him with unwelcome clarity. It comes when he's under duress. He won't say anything. He never does.

Silas felt something crack in his own calculus.

"Your Honor," he said. "May we have a brief recess?"

The judge studied him, then Henry, then Silas again.

"For what purpose?" the judge asked.

Silas didn't look away from Henry. "To consult with my client."

A pause.

"Let's take a 60-minute recess and reconvene after lunch," the judge said.

The gavel came down softly, almost politely. Henry waved him off before Silas could speak.

"I'm fine," Henry said. His voice was steady, but his hands were not. He tucked them under his thighs, hoping that hiding them would solve something.

Silas crouched beside him. "You're not fine."

Henry shook his head. "It'll pass."

"It doesn't always pass."

Silas looked at him then, really looked at him. There was no fear in his eyes. There was only resolve, and something else – an insistence that Silas recognize the cost of what he was doing.

"I suppose," Henry said, without turning, "this is where we decide what this all means."

The words were calm. There was no accusation in them, and that made them sting even more.

Silas stood beside him, looking out at the visitors who were taking photos outside of the courtroom. "Yes," he said. "It is."

Henry nodded slightly but remained seated. "I want to be clear," he said. "I don't feel blindsided."

Silas felt an instinctive urge to explain himself, sharp and immediate. He resisted it.

"It's not over, but I'm not feeling good about this right now," Henry confessed. "I knew how it might go. I knew the language and the limits." He paused. "What I didn't know was how quiet it would feel."

"I thought …" Silas stopped himself, then tried again. "I believed that if I kept the argument within their comfort, we might gain ground."

Henry finally turned to look at him. His expression was not angry. It was assessing.

"And are you satisfied?" Henry asked.

The question was simple. It left no room for abstraction.

Silas exhaled slowly. "No."

Henry studied him for a moment longer, then looked away. "That's what I thought."

They stood in silence. Helen watched them both, her expression guarded, as though waiting to see whether this exchange would fracture or hold.

Henry shifted in his seat, pausing to sip water as he swallowed a couple of aspirin during the brief exchange.

"I don't regret bringing the case," Henry said. "I need you to know that."

Silas nodded. "I'm glad."

"But," he continued, "I do regret believing that caution would cost me less."

The words hit hard.

Silas felt something in himself give way – not collapse, but open. "You are still paying the price for my restraint," he said quietly.

Henry didn't deny it. He didn't confirm it either. He simply said, "I'm carrying it because I can. That doesn't mean I should have to."

Silas nodded again, knowing the motion was inadequate.

"What happens now?" Helen asked gently.

Henry considered the question. "Now," he said, "we decide whether we accept the sense of inevitability we were feeling."

Silas looked at him. "And if we don't?"

Henry now looked directly at him. "Then you stop protecting them from discomfort," he said. "And you stop protecting yourself from consequence."

Silas felt the truth of it settle in his chest.

"I can do that," he said.

Henry stared intently before offering a deliberate nod. "That's good," he said. "I need you to do this because I can't afford you not to."

After Henry emerged from a restroom break to mop his brow, they turned, then continued back into the courtroom together, fully aligned for the first time.

The case had changed.

So had the terms under which it would continue.

When court resumed, Silas didn't return to where he had left off. He didn't devise a segue and didn't pretend continuity. He rose and placed both hands on the table.

"Your Honor," he said, "I need to correct the record."

The judge's eyebrows lifted.

Silas continued. "What I have described so far is how these systems appear to function when discussed in the abstract."

Jenkins sat up, attentive now.

"But abstraction," Silas said, "is a luxury. And like all luxuries, it is unevenly distributed."

The tone of the room shifted. Silas didn't wait for a reaction.

"There are towns in this state," he said, "where a man like my client is permitted to work during daylight hours and expected to disappear by sundown. Not by ordinance. Not by signage. By understanding."

The State's attorney was on his feet before the sentence finished.

"Objection!" he shouted.

The word rang out louder than intended. It rattled awkwardly in the room, nearly unhinged.

The judge looked at him. "On what grounds?"

The attorney opened his mouth, then closed it. He gestured vaguely, believing the objection itself could have been self-explanatory.

"Objection to …" He stopped. Tried again. "To relevance."

The judge didn't respond immediately. He glanced at Silas, then back at Jenkins.

"Denied," he said.

Jenkins didn't sit. "Your Honor, may we have a brief recess?"

The request came too quickly. It was too naked and desperate.

"For what purpose?" the judge asked.

"To …" The attorney hesitated. "To address the direction of counsel's remarks."

The judge shook his head once. "Proceed."

Silas didn't acknowledge the exchange. He had already stepped forward.

Silas sensed the opening was temporary.

The judge's pen had stopped moving. The State's attorney had nothing prepared. There was still time to narrow the argument, to return to abstraction, to let the moment pass without fracture.

Silas inhaled once, then he leaned into it.

"There are local judges," he said, "who enforce these understandings without ever writing them down."

Jenkins tried again. "Objection …"

"Denied," the judge said, sharper this time.

Silas felt the moment open in front of him – dramatic, theatrical, and exposed. He didn't slow down. It was too late to back down now.

"These judges know precisely when to look away," Silas continued. "They know which cases to call, which to delay, and which to bury in continuances until the outcome becomes inevitable without ever being announced."

And delay, he now saw, was its own form of participation.

The White half of the gallery stirred audibly now. A woman covered her mouth as she gasped.

The Negro half of the gallery came alive. Paper fans moved faster now, the rhythm unmistakable. It was not relief. It was recognition. The sound was like the opening hum of a revival, anticipation before testimony.

Jenkins stood rigid, hands braced on the table, as though physical pressure might reassert control.

Silas pressed on.

"These practices are often described as tradition," he said. "Or culture. Or order."

He looked directly at the bench.

"They are none of those things," he said. "They are enforcement."

The judge's posture stiffened, his expression no longer dispassionate.

Silas didn't stop to interpret it.

"What has been presented to this court as discretion is, in fact, precision," he said. "A calibrated system of permission and exclusion that functions without ever admitting its own design."

Silence followed. The kind that signals damage already done.

The shift tingled the entire courtroom.

The risk no longer rested with Henry Logan alone – his body, his record, or his future.

It had moved.

Onto Silas Thomas Thorn III.

And, unmistakably, onto Mississippi itself.

Jenkins moved to speak again, but the judge raised a hand.

"The record will reflect counsel's remarks in full," he said.

"Your Honor ..." Jenkins began.

"In full," the judge repeated, already turning toward the court reporter. "Proceed."

The reporter's fingers resumed their steady motion. Whatever had been said could no longer be unsaid.

As the room emptied, Henry remained seated.

He slowly stretched his fingers again, careful this time, as though testing something fragile. The pain had not vanished – it had merely quieted for now.

Helen touched his arm. Henry gave a head gesture without looking at her.

Across the aisle, Silas was already gathering his papers.

Henry watched him for a moment, then looked away, bracing himself for consequences he understood would never appear in the record.

INTERNAL MEMORANDUM
CONFIDENTIAL – NOT FOR DISTRIBUTION

To: Deputy Attorneys, Southern District
From: Office of the Attorney General, Litigation Review
Re: Logan v. Mississippi – Hearing Conduct and Forward Strategy

Date: November 8, 1965

This memorandum is intended to clarify the state's position following today's proceedings and to establish internal alignment moving forward.

During argument, plaintiff counsel departed from the anticipated scope of procedural discussion and introduced characterizations of local custom and judicial practice that, while rhetorically charged, remain legally unsupported. These remarks were delivered in a manner calculated to provoke reaction rather than advance admissible claims.

It is important to note that the court didn't adopt counsel's framing, nor did it issue any findings consistent with the implications suggested. No ruling was made concerning the existence of so-called "unwritten rules," nor was any finding entered regarding systemic enforcement outside codified law.

That said, counsel's statements were permitted to stand in the record.

This development should be understood not as judicial restraint. The court elected to allow argument to proceed rather than risk disruption. Such decisions are not uncommon and should not be misinterpreted as signaling receptiveness.

Going forward, all representatives of the state are advised to maintain strict discipline in framing. Avoid engagement with generalized sociological claims. Return consistently to jurisdiction, standing, and evidentiary relevance. Precision will be essential.

Any temptation to respond in kind – to rebut rhetoric with rhetoric – must be resisted. The strength of the state's position lies in continuity, not reaction.

Internally, however, it would be imprudent to ignore the perception risk created by today's exchange.

Accordingly:

1. All filings should be reviewed for language that could be misconstrued if read selectively or out of context.
2. No discretionary statements should be made on the record that are not strictly necessary to procedural posture.

3. External communications, if any become unavoidable, should emphasize normal course adjudication and the absence of novel legal issues.

This case does not present a threat on its merits.
Its danger lies in narrative drift.
Narratives can be corrected. Records endure.
Proceed accordingly.

***

Paul Jenkins frantically penned a handwritten note that is tight and compressed, as if compression were the same as confidentiality.

I lost control today.

Not rhetorically, but procedurally.

Thorn wasn't supposed to go there. I don't mean the towns. Everyone knows about the towns. I mean the judges.

Once he said it out loud, it changed the posture of the room. Not sympathy — attention. That's worse.

The objection came out wrong. Too loud. No grounds. The judge noticed. I could tell by the way he didn't look at me afterward.

What troubles me is not that Thorn was persuasive. It's that he didn't need to persuade. He only needed to describe.

The record is the problem.

I asked for a recess because I needed one to try to stop momentum. I could feel the floor tilt, and I didn't know where it would settle.

If this transcript leaves the building intact, we are no longer defending a case. We are defending a pattern.

I don't think the Attorney General understands that yet.

I hope I'm wrong.

        — P.J.

TWENTY-FIVE
Pressure Mounts

Word reached Silas the next morning that Henry had been admitted to the hospital overnight.

He called the court first and requested a delay. Then he called Helen.

They were back home. Henry had been released after only a few hours. His blood pressure had spiked to 178/123 – high enough that the doctors feared a stroke. They administered an injection known to bring pressure down rapidly. It had worked almost immediately. It also left him drowsy and heavy-limbed.

Silas told Helen he had asked the court for an indefinite continuance.

Before she could respond, he heard Henry in the background – raised voice, clipped cadence – objecting. Loudly. Insisting he would be back in court the next day. There was no time to waste, he said.

Everything had to be said while it could still be said, while it could still be entered into the record. Before anyone found a way to quiet the room.

Helen handed him the phone.

Henry continued without softening. It was unlike him – less measured, more insistent – but not incoherent. He was forceful, yet persuasive in a way that made interruption feel rude, so Silas listened.

Then he called the court again and updated them.

The matter would resume the following day.

***

Wednesday's hearing arrived with heightened anticipation.

Henry was already seated when Silas entered the courtroom. He sat straighter than usual, as though posture itself were a form of testimony. His jacket was buttoned despite the heat. His hands rested flat on his knees, fingers splayed slightly, not fidgeting so much as bracing. If the medication still weighed on him, he didn't allow it to show. What did show – what Silas noticed immediately – was a faint stiffness in his neck, a carefulness in the way he turned his head.

Helen was not beside him. She had chosen the back row of the gallery, near the aisle. Close enough to see him, yet far enough not to be seen as part of the proceeding.

The judge took the bench, and the clerk called the matter. Normal language, recited cleanly, like nothing had intervened. As if bodies didn't register stress. As if calendars, not people, governed the pace of justice.

Silas rose when addressed. He didn't mention the hospital. He didn't mention blood pressure, or injections, or the fact that the razor's edge between warning and consequence had narrowed overnight. He spoke only to procedure and continuation.

Across the aisle, the State's attorney listened with a polite expression that had hardened since the previous afternoon. The easy agreement was gone. He gestured less and wrote more. When Silas finished, the attorney stood and objected – not loudly this time, but thoroughly. He cited efficiency. He cited the court's schedule. He cited the danger of delay becoming precedent.

At no point did he look at Henry.

The judge considered both arguments, then ruled with a brevity that bordered on relief. The case would proceed – narrowly and carefully. Today would be limited to matters already raised. Nothing new would be introduced. Nothing expanded.

Silas acknowledged the ruling, then he sat.

Henry didn't move.

When it was his turn to be addressed – when a factual clarification required his confirmation – he rose more slowly than usual. The movement seemed to pull something tight across his shoulders. For a moment Silas thought he might steady himself against the table, but he didn't. He stood without assistance. He answered the question directly and didn't elaborate.

When he sat again, his breathing was controlled and deliberate. The courtroom returned its attention to the lawyers.

As the morning progressed, Silas became acutely aware of time – as a sequence, as much as a pressure. Each exchange felt uneasy. Each ruling landed more acutely than it should have. He caught himself abbreviating arguments he would normally refine, not out of haste, but out of calculation. The record and the order mattered. What could be undone mattered less than what could be fixed in place.

At one point during an interval, Henry shifted position and made brief eye contact.

There was no plea in the look. No instruction – only resolve and a quiet insistence that the day be used.

At the break, Silas suggested – politely – that Henry step outside, get air, and take a break.

Henry shook his head.

"Not yet," he said. His voice was steady, but lower than before. "Finish the morning."

Helen watched from the back as they returned to their places. She folded her hands together and didn't unfold them again.

By early afternoon, the judge brought the session to a close. The remaining matters would be taken up later in the week. Notices would be issued. The record would reflect what had been said.

As the courtroom emptied, Silas gathered his papers more slowly than usual. He waited until Henry stood, until he was certain he could do so without swaying. They walked out together, side by side, neither speaking until they reached the hallway.

"You didn't have to do that," Silas said at last. It was not clear which part he meant.

Henry stopped and turned to him.

"Yes," Henry said. "I did."

Then, almost as an afterthought, he added, "Tomorrow, too."

Silas watched him continue down the corridor. For the first time since the case had begun, Silas felt the unmistakable sensation that the law was not merely failing to protect his client, but was actively asking more of him than it had any right to demand.

As the next session began later that week, Silas knew he was running out of time. He had an idea that could explode or it could be explosive. Time would tell.

He turned slightly in his chair and looked at Henry – as someone who had already been navigating the terrain Silas was only beginning to understand.

"What would you do," Silas asked quietly, "if this were yours to decide?"

Henry halted before answering. He rubbed his hands together – a habit Silas had noticed when Henry was choosing his words carefully. The courtroom was emptying around them – clerks shuffling papers, the judge already gone – but Henry spoke as if the room were still full.

"I'd stop pretending this is only about what happened to me," Henry said. "Because it wasn't."

Henry glanced toward the gallery, where Helen had been sitting. She had not moved yet. She was speaking with a woman Silas didn't recognize, her face composed in the way Silas was learning was not calm but readiness.

"She's been part of this from the start," Henry continued. "Just not on paper."

Silas thought deeply. For months he had treated Helen Logan as context – important, present, but legally peripheral. The realization landed softly, which was how Silas now recognized the most consequential shifts.

"She should testify," Silas said.

Henry looked straight into his eyes. Instead of surprise, he saw nothing but a sense of relief.

"As an expert," Silas added.

Henry exhaled loudly. "That'll upset them."

Silas allowed himself to smile a slight smile. "Yes. It will."

***

The objection came exactly as Silas expected it would.

The State's attorney, Jenkins, rose with his now-expected irritation. "Your Honor, this is highly irregular. Mrs. Logan is not a medical professional. She is not a sociologist. She is not qualified to offer expert testimony."

Silas stood before the judge could respond.

"She is uniquely qualified," Silas said, his voice even, "because expertise is not limited to those who study harm. Some people survive it."

Jenkins scoffed audibly. "With respect, counsel is attempting to smuggle emotion into an evidentiary record."

Silas turned slightly – not toward Jenkins, but toward the bench.

"Mrs. Logan has done more than witness the consequences of these policies," he said. "She absorbed them, managed them, and she anticipated them."

He paused.

"She monitored my client's health when medical care was inaccessible. She rationed food when routes were unpredictable. She packed and repacked their lives to remain mobile, compliant, and invisible. She did this while raising two young children. She did this without the luxury of outrage."

Silas noticed the atmosphere in the room become calm and motionless.

"She was his support system, his nurse, his nutritionist, and the face that had to reassure their children that this was normal – that some fears are simply part of adulthood."

Jenkins gasped.

Silas finished quietly. "If the court is interested in understanding the full scope of the harm, it cannot pretend she was incidental."

The judge studied the file, then Jenkins.

Jenkins straightened his jacket. "The State withdraws its objection."

He smiled as he sat down – not apologetic or gracious. Just annoyed.

***

Lorraine arrived in the gallery about the same time that Silas and Henry were trying to make eye contact with Helen.

She took a seat on the Negro side of the gallery, careful not to disturb the women already seated there.

The courtroom was smaller than she had imagined. Not intimate, exactly, but contained, like a place designed to limit the amount of trouble that could occur inside it.

She had come to quietly support Henry.

She found him easily. He sat at the counsel table, posture straight, eyes fixed forward with a discipline that looked practiced. He didn't look like a man on trial so much as a man enduring something he had already decided not to react to.

Then the man beside him shifted.

Lorraine followed the movement and felt the recognition arrive before the name did. The angle of his shoulders. The way he held himself used motion as a form of speech.

Silas.

He had failed to tell her his last name when they last saw each other, but she knew it was the same man.

The realization unsettled her because of what his presence meant. She had assumed Henry was being represented. She had not assumed it would be by *him*.

As if in response to the thought, Silas glanced up.

Their eyes met only briefly. Not long enough to be acknowledged, but long enough for certainty. His expression didn't change. He didn't wave. He returned his attention to the bench as though the moment had never occurred.

Lorraine understood right away. This was not a place for recognition. Not even for reassurance. Whatever role Silas was playing here required an undeniable kind of distance.

She looked back at Henry.

He had not turned. He had not looked for anyone. He sat as he had been sitting, already inside the machinery of the proceeding, already bearing its weight.

Lorraine dutifully faced forward, her red ribbon unseen from this angle.

The trial continued, as Helen took the stand.

She raised a shaky hand as she was sworn to tell the truth and nothing else. Her voice didn't quiver at first.

The truth. All of it, or the parts that wouldn't destroy them further?

She spoke of the Green Book like it was a household tool – no different than a wrench or a flashlight. Something you kept close as an emergency utility.

"We planned our trips around it," she said. "Not the distance. The fringes."

What she didn't say: how Henry studied those pages like scripture. How he traced routes with his finger before they left, memorizing distances between safe stops because stopping wrong could mean not arriving. How she watched him do this and said nothing about the tightness in his jaw, because naming his fear would make it more real for the children.

She described keeping a bag packed in the hall closet that was not for vacations. It was for leaving quickly.

"Shoes already inside," she said. "For all of us."

The State's attorney was writing this down. Good. That meant it was useful. That meant her life was translating into evidence correctly.

She spoke of fuel gauges and the quiet panic of unexpected detours. Of teaching children to remain silent when adults were tense.

What she couldn't say: how many times she'd gently and urgently placed her hand on Daniel's mouth. A mother's touch that meant this silence might save you. How her daughter learned to read her face for danger before she could read words. How normal this became. How she taught them to survive and hated herself for needing to.

Then her voice quivered.

She felt it before she heard it. The break in her own testimony.

Henry was watching. She couldn't look at him. If she looked at him, she would see him hearing these things – things he knew but had never heard her say aloud to strangers. She would see him understanding that their marriage was being examined, their strategies catalogued, their survival methods transformed into legal exhibits.

Silas had told her this would help. That her lived experience was expertise. But expertise suggested mastery, and she had mastered nothing. She had only endured.

"You learn not to hope for ease," Helen said. "You hope for predictability."

"And even that," she added, "was never guaranteed."

This was the part she had rehearsed. The part that explained without accusing. The part that made White people understand without making them responsible.

But even as she said it, she was calculating: Would this sentence protect Henry or expose him more? Would naming how they lived make the court see the system's violence, or would it mark them as the kind of Negroes who didn't know their place?

The State's attorney was watching her with a face that looked neutral, but she recognized as assessment. He was deciding if she was credible. If her tears were authentic. If her testimony was exaggerated.

She was being graded on her own suffering.

Nuremberg, Mississippi

The courtroom was silent.

No one interrupted her. Not the State, and not the court.

She should feel relief. The testimony was going well. Silas seemed satisfied.

But sitting here, performing her life for legal consumption, Helen felt something else – the awareness that she was building the case that would make Henry more visible. Every word she spoke was evidence, yes. But it was also exposure.

She was testifying about the Green Book, about the packed bags, about teaching her children fear as a survival skill. She was making their strategies public. And when this trial ended, they would still be in Mississippi – more visible than before, more identified, more known to the people who made the Green Book necessary in the first place.

Silas thought he was giving her a voice.

What he was giving her was a permanent record of how she had survived. A record that would follow Henry. That would mark them. That would confirm to anyone paying attention that the Logans were the kind of Negroes who challenged things.

She wondered if Silas understood that his careful legal strategy required her to speak openly in a system that punished her people for being too visible. That restraint in the courtroom meant exposure outside it.

She wondered if Henry understood that she was doing this because she loved him, even though doing it might cost him more than staying silent would have.

She wondered if her children would someday read this testimony and understand why their mother had described their childhood to strangers. Or if they would only see that she had made their private terrors public.

Jenkins asked another question.

Helen steadied her voice and answered.

She was an expert witness now. An expert in survival. An expert in unpredictability. An expert in teaching children to be afraid correctly.

She answered each question with the same careful calibration she used for everything – what could be said safely. What would sound credible to White ears. What would help Henry without endangering him further.

She was performing restraint while testifying about the necessity of restraint.

The irony was not lost on her. But irony was not admissible as evidence.

So, she continued. She translated her life into legal language. She made her marriage into testimony. She turned her children's fear into exhibits.

And she did not look at Henry, because if she looked at him, she would see him calculating whether this was worth it. Whether her testimony was helping or simply making them more vulnerable.

She kept her eyes forward and finished what she had been asked to do.

When she stepped down from the stand, she did not feel victorious. She felt like she had just testified against her own family's safety.

But Silas smiled slightly as she passed, and she understood that her performance had been successful.

The court had found her credible, which meant her suffering had been presented in an acceptable format.

Which meant the case could continue. That meant Henry would remain exposed.

She returned to her seat in the gallery and finally allowed herself to look at her husband. Lorraine was in tears, as was every other woman in the Negro section of the gallery.

Henry was not looking at Helen. He was looking at the table in front of him, his shoulders carrying a weight she recognized but could not name in any language the court would understand.

She had done what was asked of her.

Now they would both live with the consequences of her cooperation.

TWENTY-SIX
News in Black and White

THE JACKSON CLARION-LEDGER

MISSISSIPPI COURT HEARS EXPANDED TESTIMONY IN LOCAL DISPUTE

Federal proceedings continued Tuesday in the matter of Logan v. Mississippi, with the court permitting testimony from a family member of the plaintiff. Attorneys for the State expressed concern over the precedent such testimony could set but ultimately deferred to the court's discretion.

Observers noted an emotional tone during portions of the hearing, though legal analysts emphasized that the case remains centered on procedural questions rather than allegations of misconduct.

The court has not indicated when a ruling may be expected.

THE MISSISSIPPI FREE VOICE

"WE PACKED TO RUN": WIFE TESTIFIES IN FEDERAL COURT

Helen Logan stood before a federal judge yesterday and described a life shaped by preparation – bags packed, routes mapped, children trained to be quiet when danger approached unexpectedly.

Her testimony took Logan v. Mississippi from an abstract dispute over ordinances, to a daily negotiation for survival. Speaking calmly and without embellishment, Logan detailed the cost of living under laws that required constant vigilance.

"She wasn't emotional," said one observer. "She was precise."

The court allowed the testimony over initial objection from the State.

THE JACKSON CLARION-LEDGER

STATE QUESTIONS RELEVANCE OF PERSONAL EXPERIENCE

State attorneys reiterated their position that anecdotal testimony risks obscuring the legal issues at stake. "Courts are not forums for personal narratives," one source close to the case stated.

Nonetheless, the testimony was entered into the record.

THE MISSISSIPPI FREE VOICE

EXPERTISE WITHOUT A TITLE

Helen Logan didn't claim credentials. She claimed memory.

She spoke of fuel levels and back roads. Of teaching children not to ask why they couldn't stop. Of a bag kept ready – not for convenience, but necessity.

If expertise is measured by repetition, endurance, and consequence, then the court heard from one of the most qualified witnesses it has ever seated.

The morning after Helen Logan testified, the papers arrived folded the same way they always had.

In Jackson, men in pressed shirts opened the Clarion-Ledger at the counter of the King Edward café, scanning headlines between spoonfuls of grits and bacon. One man tapped the page with his finger.

"Same case again," he said. "Still going."

Another shrugged. "Federal court likes to drag things out."

A waitress refilled cups without slowing. No one asked what the testimony had been. No one wondered who had spoken.

"Sounds like a family matter," a third man said. "Probably shouldn't have been federal to begin with."

They turned the page.

***

Across town, the Mississippi Free Voice lay open on a table sticky with syrup and cigarette ash. The café was smaller and louder, less careful about who overheard what.

"She talked about keeping a bag packed," a woman said, her fork paused mid-air. "For her kids."

A man beside her shook his head slowly. "That ain't testimony. That's a warning."

Someone laughed because laughter was easier than saying what everyone already understood.

"They printed every word," the woman added. "That never happens."

"That's because nobody can say she's lying," the man said. "They just don't want to say she's right."

***

By afternoon, the story had migrated – dissected and altered.

In a barber shop off Capitol Street, a radio murmured about the hearing while clippers buzzed. The barber leaned close to a customer's ear.

"They let the wife talk," he said. "That's new."

The customer frowned. "About what?"

"Life," the barber replied. "Which is why they'll pretend it didn't happen."

They shared a look that didn't require elaboration.

***

That night, the juke joint outside Yazoo City was crowded, the air thick with sweat and sound. The case came up between songs.

"I heard she said she never let the tank get below half," a man said, shouting over the music.

A woman shook her head. "No. She said she never trusted a full one either."

That hit everyone hard.

Someone fed another coin into the machine. The music resumed. The conversation didn't.

***

Miles away, in a quiet living room with the television turned low, a couple sat with the Clarion-Ledger folded neatly on the arm of a chair.

"They're making it emotional," the woman said, glancing at the paper without opening it.

"That's how they do," the man replied. "Turn everything into a sideshow."

Neither could have said what the testimony was.

***

What passed for coverage depended entirely on where you stood.

In some rooms, Helen Logan had testified.

In others, a procedural irregularity had occurred.

In many, nothing at all had happened.

The stories didn't argue with each other. They didn't even collide. They simply occupied different territories, like weather systems that never meet.

And so the state continued its day — each half convinced it understood the other, neither aware of how little it knew.

The separation didn't announce itself as conflict.

It appeared instead as confidence.

***

By evening, the case had become something people knew about without knowing.

In a roadside café west of Meridian, a waitress said, "They're saying it's about travel now."

A trucker laughed. "Everything's about travel if you let it be."

She refilled his coffee. "You ever plan a trip you weren't sure you'd finish?"

He didn't answer. He stirred his cup until the sound of the spoon stopped.

***

What astonished Silas — though he would not articulate it until much later – was not that people disagreed about the case.

It was that they were not disagreeing about the same thing.

Some were debating federal overreach.

Some were recounting survival techniques.

Some were repeating talking points.

Some were revisiting memories they had trained themselves not to name.

The words Logan v. Mississippi referred to all of it and none of it, depending on who spoke to them and where.

***

By the end of the week, the papers had moved on.

The Clarion-Ledger replaced the story with an editorial about judicial restraint.

The Free Voice ran a photograph of Helen Logan leaving the courthouse, her expression unreadable, the caption plain.

In cafes and juke joints, the case receded unresolved and absorbed into existing knowledge, where it could no longer disrupt anything.

That was how the state protected itself. Not by denying what had been said. But by ensuring that no single room ever heard all of it at once.

TWENTY-SEVEN
Chambers

Judge Mathewson closed the door to his chambers and loosened his tie.

The hearing had ended two hours ago, but the transcript still sat on his desk, Thorn's words underlined in three places.

He had allowed the testimony. That had been correct procedurally. A wife's perspective on enforcement patterns was arguably relevant to disparate impact analysis.

But he had also felt something shift in the gallery. The way sound had changed when Helen Logan spoke about packing bags. The way even Jenkins had gone quiet.

Mathewson had spent thirty years believing that fairness meant applying the same rules to everyone. But what if the rules themselves...

He stopped the thought. While pouring himself bourbon, he noticed a photograph on his wall of him shaking hands with Senator Eastland at his swearing-in.

The system worked because judges didn't ask those questions.

He locked the transcript in his desk drawer and went to have dinner before going home.

TWENTY-EIGHT
A Woman Scorned

Even a quiet table in the corner no longer provided solitude.

Silas had stopped for lunch in a town he didn't know well, choosing the place for anonymity. The café was clean and quiet, the kind of place designed to keep conversations from lingering.

He took a seat near the window, set his briefcase at his feet, and unfolded the paper.

Two men occupied the table behind him. Their voices were low, unguarded in the way people speak when they believe the subject is resolved.

"They let the wife testify," one said.

"That so?"

"Yeah. Don't see how that holds up."

"It won't," the other replied. "Judges indulge that kind of thing sometimes. Makes everyone feel heard."

Silas kept his eyes on the page.

"Whole thing's getting blown out of proportion," the first man continued. "It's a local issue. Always was."

The second man laughed softly. "Federal court's just theater."

Silas felt the familiar reflex – the one honed by years of classrooms and courtrooms – to correct, to clarify, to impose order on a misstatement before it hardened into fact.

He didn't this time.

The waitress approached. "Are you ready to order?"

"Yes," he said, pointing to the menu special of the day.

She refilled his water glass. The men behind him moved on to another topic without transition, as though the case had concluded simply by being dismissed aloud.

Silas folded the paper.

What troubled him was not the casual tone. He had heard worse. It was the efficiency of it, the way Helen's testimony had been reduced to indulgence, stripped of labor, memory, and consequence in less than a minute.

The men had not rejected the testimony.

They had never received it.

Helen lived it.

***

She changed her path even before there was any reason to do so.

Initially, she offered no explanation. She simply began to leave earlier and return later, opting for longer roads that avoided intersections. Even on days when Henry anticipated being home by noon, she packed lunches.

When he inquired about the changes, she merely replied, "It's easier this way."

She no longer allowed the children to walk to the neighbor's house by themselves. She started answering the phone on the second ring instead of the first. The Green Book was moved from the hall table to the kitchen drawer, closer to her usual spot.

Henry took notice.

"You don't have to do all this yet," he remarked one evening, making an effort not to sound ungrateful.

"I know," Helen responded.

That was the extent of their conversation.

Two days later, a truck lingered behind Henry longer than necessary before passing him by. The driver didn't make eye contact.

The following week, a clerk misplaced paperwork that had never gone missing before. It was later found, intact, as if it had wandered off on its own.

Helen said nothing.

By the time the call came through – concerning an erroneous warning and a misunderstanding requiring explanation – she had already changed the schedule. As a result, Henry was not in the location they expected.

That evening, after the children had fallen asleep, Henry quietly stated, "You saw this coming."

Helen folded a towel and placed it neatly in the drawer. "I recognized the pattern," she replied. "That's all."

Later, in his car, Silas sat with the engine off, the briefcase unopened beside him. He thought of Henry's hands – how they had rested on his knees when he spoke, steady because he had practiced steadiness for years.

He thought of Helen's voice when it thinned, soft, yet precise.

And he understood something he had resisted throughout the case.

The law didn't merely sort facts.

It decided which lives required translation and which were already legible.

Silas had believed, for too long, that his role was to make the case intelligible – to render injustice in terms the system could recognize without recoiling.

Helen had done something else entirely.

She had spoken without translation.

And the system, when faced with that clarity, had simply routed it elsewhere.

When Silas finally left the cafe, he didn't turn toward the courthouse.

He drove in the opposite direction, unsure of where he was going, but certain of what he could no longer do.

He could not pretend that success in court meant understanding had occurred.

He could not confuse admission into the record with entry into memory.

And he could no longer tell himself that restraint was impartial.

The case would proceed, the briefs would be filed, and the opinion would come.

But something irreversible had already happened.

The distance between what had been said and what could be heard had become the case itself.

And Silas knew – quietly, definitively – that no ruling could close that gap.

TWENTY-NINE
Judgment Day

**UNITED STATES DISTRICT COURT
FOR THE SOUTHERN DISTRICT OF MISSISSIPPI**

Henry Logan,
Plaintiff,

v.

State of Mississippi,
Defendant.

Civil Action No. ___

MEMORANDUM OPINION AND ORDER

Nuremberg, Mississippi

B efore the Court is the plaintiff's complaint alleging violations of his constitutional rights arising from actions taken by local authorities within the State of Mississippi. The plaintiff seeks declaratory and injunctive relief, asserting that the challenged practices unlawfully burdened his freedom of movement and equal protection under the law.

The Court has reviewed the pleadings, the evidentiary record, and the arguments presented by counsel. For the reasons set forth below, the Court finds that relief is not warranted.

I. Background

The plaintiff, Henry Logan, is a resident of this district who alleges that he was subjected to restrictions imposed by local officials that limited his presence within certain municipal boundaries after nightfall. The plaintiff contends that these restrictions, though not formalized by statute, operated with sufficient regularity and authority to constitute State action in violation of his constitutional rights.

The defendant does not dispute that the plaintiff experienced inconvenience and distress as a result of the encounters giving rise to this action. The defendant argues, however, that the conduct at issue fell within the scope of local discretion historically afforded to municipal authorities, and that no enforceable federal right was infringed.

II. Findings

The Court does not question the sincerity of the plaintiff's account, nor does it dismiss the historical context in which such encounters arise. The record reflects that Mr. Logan experienced a tangible burden on his freedom of movement, and that this burden was not trivial in its effect.

The Court further recognizes that informal practices, when repeated and unexamined, may produce consequences that warrant serious concern. Such concerns, however, do not alone determine the outcome of this case.

The role of this Court is not to evaluate the wisdom of local custom, nor to remedy every harm that arises at the margins of lawful discretion. Federal jurisdiction is limited, and the Constitution does not guarantee freedom from all forms of discomfort, indignity, or unequal experience.

To prevail, the plaintiff must demonstrate that the challenged conduct exceeded the authority granted to local officials under controlling precedent, or that it constituted a clear and enforceable violation of federal law. On the record before it, the Court cannot make that finding.

III. Legal Analysis

The plaintiff urges the Court to treat the conduct at issue as a de facto policy attributable to the State. While the Court acknowledges the force of this argument, it finds that the evidentiary showing falls short of establishing a practice sufficiently definite and uniform to warrant federal intervention.

The absence of formal codification, while not dispositive, limits the Court's ability to impose prospective relief without venturing beyond its proper role. The Court is mindful that judicial restraint is not indifference, but a recognition of institutional boundaries.

This case presents serious questions. It does not, however, present a justiciable basis upon which this Court may grant the relief requested.

IV. Conclusion

The Court acknowledges the seriousness of the plaintiff's concerns and the reality of the burden he describes. Recognition of harm, however, does not compel judicial remedy in the absence of a clear violation within the Court's authority to correct.

Accordingly, the plaintiff's request for declaratory and injunctive relief is **DENIED**.

Judgment is entered for the defendants.

This matter is **DISMISSED WITH PREJUDICE**.

SO ORDERED, this 5th day of December, 1965

Judge T. William Mathewson
United States District Judge

THIRTY
Window Closes

Attorney and client didn't speak during the waiting period because anything he might say would still be provisional. Silas had learned, over time, that clients heard certainty where lawyers offered process, and he was no longer willing to confuse the two.

The decision had arrived already bound and complete. It didn't invite response. It invited observation.

Silas watched the days instead.

He tracked them quietly. He didn't circle dates or make notes in the margins. He paid attention to the things that usually accompanied continuation – and noticed their absence. No request for transcripts. No calls asking about timing. No signs that anyone was preparing to carry the matter forward.

The case didn't expand outward. It remained exactly where it had been left.

He reread the opinion several times, then put it away. He was not looking for error. He was looking for posture. What he saw was care – not care for the plaintiff, but care for containment. The language didn't defend. It declined to move.

That, more than the holding, told him what would follow.

Silas had once believed that appeal windows existed to preserve possibility. He understood now that they also served another function: they allowed time for consensus to form without being spoken. When no one moved, the stillness became agreement.

On the twenty-ninth day, he noticed that he had stopped expecting anything to happen.

On the thirtieth, he understood why.

The appeal period ended without a memorandum being circulated. No one asked whether a filing was still possible. The calendar advanced. When the State's attorney unlocked his office that morning, the file sat where he had left it, unmarked by any sign of reconsideration.

Thirty-one days had passed. That was enough. Jenkins didn't review the rules again. He had known, even while the hearings were underway, how the matter would end if it ended quietly.

This was not a result worth celebrating. It preserved no new ground. It simply avoided loss. He understood the difference.

He locked the file away rather than returning it to the shelf. Some matters were finished by being contained.

Life at the courthouse resumed as usual. The phones continued to ring, and clerks walked through the hallways. There was no sign anywhere in the building that a verdict had been reached.

He turned off the light and left.

PART VI: AFTERMATH

THIRTY-ONE
Henry Logan's Private Reaction

At home on the night of the ruling, Henry didn't tell anyone if he had won.

He sat at the small kitchen table with the radio off and the lights dimmed, reading the order again. He was determined to understand what it had not said.

No apology.

No recognition.

No instruction to stop.

Just permission – for the question to exist.

Helen asked if it was good news.

"It's news," he said.

He traced the margin of the paper with his finger, stopping where the judge had written that the Constitution didn't turn on labels. He liked that sentence. It sounded true in a way that didn't ask for agreement.

Still, nothing about tonight was different.

If he stepped outside after dark, the same rules would find him. If he were stopped, the same questions would be asked. The road would not know what had happened in that courtroom.

But something else had shifted.

For the first time, the thing that had always hovered – unnamed, unarguable – had been written down as something that acted. Not a rumor or a warning. An action.

"You know," Henry said to Helen, "… when they ruled against me, it never felt personal."

A short breath.

"It felt like it had always felt – unemotional and detached."

He stopped there, then added more quietly:

"I'm not saying Thorn wanted that. Only that sometimes the system looks a lot like an agreement from where I stand."

Henry realized that nothing could return what he'd lost, and accepting this was something he would have to live with.

He folded the order and placed it back in the envelope.

A man could live a long time on less than justice, he thought.

But not forever.

THIRTY-TWO
Silas Thorn's Realization

At midnight on one of his last nights at the hotel, Silas stood by the window.

The ruling lay on the desk behind him, face down, as if even looking at it required a posture he hadn't earned.

He had won the only way the law ever truly allowed him to win – by narrowing the question until it could no longer refuse to answer. No declarations. Just exposure.

And yet.

Henry had rubbed his hands during the hearing, a small movement, barely visible unless you knew to watch for it. Silas had seen it. He had chosen not to stop.

He told himself – again – that this was how protection worked. That delay was safety. That escalation could wait.

The system would respond. It always did.

It wasn't the ruling that bothered him the most. It was how easily everything returned to routine afterward.

Silas understood then – not as theory, but as fact – that abstraction had cost Henry something already. Not all at once and not dramatically.

In increments.

Silas sat on the edge of the bed and finally turned the order over. The words had not changed. But they no longer felt clean.

It was occurring to him that what he had long called neutrality might simply have been comfort wearing a cloak they called restraint.

He had believed that reducing harm was the same as opposing it.

Tonight, once again, he was reminded of the difference.

THIRTY-THREE
Fishing Buddies

enry didn't call it running away.

He called it practical.

The first incident was a brick through the front window at three in the morning, the sound sharp enough to pull Henry upright before the glass finished falling. He stood in the hallway with his bare feet on the cold floor, listening for a second noise that didn't come. Helen turned on the lamp in the bedroom and looked at him without speaking. Their children didn't wake, and that, in a strange way, made it worse. The house absorbed the violence the way it would if it had been weather.

The second incident arrived as silence. His supervisor stopped answering. A promise of overtime vanished. A man he had worked beside for three years began to look through him in the yard as if Henry had become a ghost.

Nuremberg, Mississippi

He told himself to keep his voice level. To keep his hands steady. To not hand anyone the satisfaction of watching him flinch.

Then the tire went flat in the church parking lot.

He noticed it before anyone else did because he had begun to notice everything. He crouched beside the wheel, ran his thumb along the rubber, and found the clean cut. The blade had been sharp. Whoever did it wanted him to know it could be done quickly.

That night, Helen sat at the kitchen table after the children were asleep and began to sort papers into piles that made sense only to her – birth certificates, school records, a folded deed. She didn't ask him whether they were leaving. She arranged the future as if the decision had already been made, because in truth it had.

Henry watched her hands. He understood that the choice was no longer about pride.

Leaving was not surrender. Leaving was the only way to keep the children from learning the wrong lessons.

They moved without a public goodbye. No one would have called it forced. They would have called it a change, a personal decision, or a family relocating for opportunity. Henry didn't correct anyone. He let the euphemisms do their work. He had learned what happened to men who insisted on proper names.

The new town didn't know his face. That helped. He found work that was not better, only different – hands-on and steady. He learned which streets stayed lit. Which stores closed early. Which cashier's expression tightened when his change touched her palm.

In Mississippi, he had learned the rules by living inside them. Here, he learned them by watching.

It was calmer, and the calm came with its own kind of alertness, like a body that has stopped expecting the blow but cannot stop preparing for it.

Silas stayed in contact.

At first the calls were cautious. Henry kept them practical – addresses, school registrations, whether the job would hold, whether the landlord seemed decent. Silas listened more than he spoke. He asked questions the way a lawyer asks questions, but not in the old voice. Not like Henry were evidence.

Over time, the calls changed. They became less about survival and more about connection. Fishing and other ordinary matters men reach for when they are trying to treat each other as neighbors rather than artifacts of a case.

One March afternoon in 1969, Silas said he would be passing through and asked whether Henry wanted to go fishing.

Henry waited before answering. The invitation felt almost naïve, as if the world were safe enough to justify it. But it also felt like an attempt to return them to something simpler than their shared history. Henry agreed before he could talk himself out of it.

He chose the spot.

A small public stretch of water behind an overgrown stand of willow trees, where no one asked questions. Men came, cast a line, and minded their own business. It was the sort of place where solitude didn't look suspicious.

They arrived early enough that the air still carried the morning dew. Henry brought a modest tackle box and two folding chairs.

Silas basically brought the Sears and Roebuck catalog.

"Come on, man," Henry chuckled. "You brought enough food for three trips. That new fishing hat makes you look like you read a manual on how to be a person outside a courthouse."

Silas sheepishly took off his hat, which ruffled his hair. He then slapped the hat onto Henry's head, leading to a moment of stunning unguardedness.

They set their chairs closer together than either could have planned. The distance between them was humanized by a hat and some laughter.

The water moved in soft increments. Small ripples. A slow current. The sun climbing and the birds chorusing.

Silas cast first. The line made a clean arc and landed with a quiet plop. He watched the bobber with the concentration of a man who had spent too long watching juries.

Henry waited a moment longer before casting. He let the line go out slowly, feeling the weight settle. The act steadied him. The stillness did something inside his ribs, loosening a tension he had stopped noticing.

They didn't talk about Mississippi. They didn't talk about the case.

The silence was not awkward. It was earned.

After a while, Silas looked down at his hands and said, almost casually, "I never learned the knots right."

Henry glanced at him. Silas's tone tried for lightness, but the admission carried more than it should have. A man who knew how to cross-examine witnesses didn't want to admit he couldn't tie a simple line.

Henry opened his tackle box, pulled out a spare hook, and reached for Silas's line.

"Here," he said.

He worked slowly, deliberately, letting his fingers do what they remembered. The motion was familiar enough to feel like borrowed time. He patiently showed Silas the steps, because the point was not speed. The point was that something held.

He had learned that anything tied too tightly failed first.

Silas followed along without correcting him. Without insisting. He let Henry teach, and Henry felt a quiet satisfaction that had nothing to do with fish.

When a breeze moved through the reeds, the surface of the water tightened and then smoothed again. The world remained unbothered.

They caught very little. A small bass Henry threw back. A sunfish Silas held up as if it were a prize and then released with exaggerated care, as though he didn't want to be seen harming anything.

Around mid-day, they ate sandwiches and drank from the cooler. Silas asked about the children. Henry answered in short, factual sentences, the way he always did when speaking about what he loved most – protecting it by not offering it to the world's appetite, even Silas.

"I got married," Silas said, tired of waiting for the right moment. "To someone I met in Jackson."

"What's her name," Henry asked.

"Her name is Lorraine," Silas said. "Lorraine Bishop."

"The woman from the Tip Top?"

Silas merely nodded. Henry was quiet for a long moment. Then he stood, set down his rod, and tightly embraced Silas.

"Good job, my brother."

That's when something began to make sense to him.

"She was at the trial," Henry said. "In the gallery. Red ribbon."

Silas looked at him, startled. "You saw her?"

"I thought she was there to support me after reading about the case in the paper," Henry said. "After she recognized you, I think that's why she came back after the break."

They were quiet for a moment.

"She told me once," Silas said, "that she watched me hesitate before dancing with her. Said it looked like I was calculating whether it was safe."

Henry's smile faded. "And what did you tell her?"

"That I was."

"And what did she say?"

Silas cast his line again. "She said she already knew. That's why she didn't wait for me to ask her first."

Henry found he could accept that.

They sat again and watched the water.

Henry became aware, slowly, that his shoulders had dropped. That his jaw was unclenched.

On the drive home, Henry noticed he kept expecting something to interrupt the day, wondering if his peace required an explanation. He didn't name the feeling. He didn't trust it enough to honor it with a title.

***

The morning it happened, Henry drove alone.

The road was familiar. He knew where it curved. Where the trees narrowed the light. He was thinking about nothing when his hands tightened – not quite pain – just resistance, as though the tendons had forgotten their roles.

He swallowed. The swallow didn't finish.

He told himself nothing. His thoughts didn't organize.

The road widened, then narrowed. His grip felt approximate. Present, but misplaced.

The truck drifted.

He corrected, or believed he did. The wheel moved, but the road didn't respond. There was a brief sensation – not fear – of being carried by his own arms.

His foot searched and found resistance too late.

The trees came closer.

He had the clear impulse to slow, to wait for the feeling to pass. It didn't.

The truck left the road and met the tree with a sound that interrupted rather than exploded. Metal folded and glass webbed. The vehicle stopped.

It stopped against the old hanging tree just off the shoulder, its trunk thick, its lower branches long since cut away. It had stood there longer than the road.

The radiator steamed and the engine went quiet.

Nuremberg, Mississippi

THIRTY-FOUR
The Hanging Tree

The notice arrived before the explanation.

It came by telephone, not from the sheriff's office but from a dispatcher who worked there – someone who had learned to speak carefully, who had learned that certain sentences carried weight whether they were spoken plainly or not.

There had been an accident.

Henry Logan had been driving alone. No other vehicles were involved. He had left town earlier than usual, taking the county road rather than the highway. Somewhere past the bend near the old church property, his truck left the pavement and struck a tree.

They believed it had been a medical event. A stroke, most likely. There were no skid marks. No attempt to brake. No indication that he had seen the tree before he reached it.

By the time anyone arrived, Henry was already gone.

The tree stood exactly where it always had.

None of the details mattered much. Still, they were offered. The road curved gently there, designed to slow traffic, as though offering time to correct a mistake. Henry didn't correct it.

Later, the coroner would write that death was caused by natural means, compounded by impact. The report would be signed, filed, and closed. The tree would not be mentioned.

Someone – no one knew who – remembered what the tree had once been used for.

Not officially. Not in any document that mattered. Just a recollection passed between two men standing at the edge of the road, their hats removed out of reverence.

"That one?" one of them asked.

"Yes," the other said.

And that was all.

Helen was told that Henry had not suffered. That the stroke would have come suddenly. That he would not have known what was happening. The words were offered gently, as though they could sooth something.

Helen asked if she could see him.

The dispatcher's voice changed – softer, almost apologetic.

"Ma'am, given the circumstances... I'd recommend remembering him as he was."

Helen understood what wasn't being said. She thanked him and hung up the phone.

Only then did her knees give out.

The children were not home yet. The house was quiet in the particular way it had become since the trial – quiet not from peace, but from vigilance. Helen sat at the kitchen table and placed both hands flat against the surface, carefully bracing herself.

Henry had taken that road before. He preferred it. Said it gave him time to think.

She wondered, briefly and without judgment, whether he had known where he was when his body failed him. Whether the place had registered. Whether the past had arrived before the pain.

The thought didn't stay long.

The file was closed on a Tuesday.

Cause of death noted. Jurisdiction transferred. Pending actions marked moot.

The notation required three signatures. All were provided.

No disciplinary review was triggered, and no procedural irregularity identified. The matter didn't meet the threshold for escalation. Records were retained in accordance with policy.

By the time Silas learned of Henry's death, the facts had already reconciled into their final shape. There was nothing to argue with. Nothing to contest. No one to blame.

A stroke. A tree. An end.

The tree would remain standing like it always had.

The Myrtle County Ledger

June 14, 1969

Local Man Dies in Single-Vehicle Accident

A local man was killed Tuesday morning in a one-vehicle automobile accident on a county road outside of town.

According to authorities, the vehicle left the roadway and struck a tree. No other cars were involved. Officials believe the incident may have been caused by a medical event.

The driver was pronounced dead at the scene.

The Delta Sentinel

June 14, 1969 – Front Page Editorial

Henry Logan Didn't Live Long. He Lived Brave.

Henry Logan died yesterday morning at the age of thirty-four.

The official notice will say he was taken by a sudden illness. It will say his truck struck a tree. It will say there were no other parties involved.

That language is precise.

It is also incomplete.

Henry Logan was a husband, a father, and a laborer who understood – long before many of us did – that the law could injure as quietly as it could protect. When faced with rules designed to keep him small, invisible, and compliant, Henry did something rare.

He stood alone.

He didn't do so because he believed he would win. He didn't do so because the outcome promised him comfort, safety, or reward. He did so because the wrongness of the thing had become heavier than the risk of naming it.

The case that bore his name will never restore what it cost him. The law he challenged was never aimed at his benefit. He knew that. He proceeded anyway.

That kind of courage is easy to misunderstand, especially by those who never had to practice it.

Henry Logan was only thirty-four years old. He leaves behind a wife who carried more fear than she was ever meant to, children who will grow up knowing their father's name before they fully understand his choice, and a community that owes him more than silence.

History often remembers victories. It rarely remembers those who acted without the promise of one.

We remember Henry Logan today because he refused to pretend.

Some fights do not save the fighter. They save the truth.

And sometimes, that has to be enough.

THIRTY-FIVE
The Unfinished Conversation

Silas drove to the funeral though Helen had not invited him.

The church was small, wooden, and full. He stood in the back, near the door, where White visitors stood when they came to pay respects, present but not presuming.

He didn't approach Helen or the children. He stood through the service and listened.

The pastor spoke of Henry's steadiness. Of his skill. Of the way he taught his children to measure twice and cut once, because precision mattered.

A neighbor spoke about the time Henry repaired her fence after a storm, refusing payment.

Another man – one Silas didn't recognize – spoke about Henry's laughter. How rare it was and how full it was when it came.

No one mentioned the case.

No one mentioned Mississippi.

No one mentioned Silas.

He understood this was deliberate. The case had taken enough. It would not take the funeral, too.

Afterward, as people filed out, Helen saw him.

She didn't approach immediately. She finished speaking with an older woman, embraced her, then turned and walked toward him with that same careful posture he had seen at the courthouse – steady, deliberate, and refusing to rush.

"Mr. Thorn," she said.

"Mrs. Logan." His voice caught. "I'm sorry. I'm so sorry."

She studied him for a long moment.

"You stayed," she said finally.

"Not enough," he said.

"No," Helen agreed. "But you stayed."

She reached into her purse and removed a folded piece of paper.

"Henry wrote this," she said. "After the last hearing. Before – " She didn't finish the thought.

"He wanted you to have it if something happened," Helen said. "Not because he predicted this. Because he believed in being prepared."

Silas unfolded it.

The handwriting was Henry's – careful and practiced, the same handwriting from the repair estimates and permit applications.

Silas,

If you're reading this, I'm gone. And if I'm gone the way I think I might be – not dramatically, just finally – then there are some things you need to know.

You asked me once why I didn't seem angry.

I was. I am. But anger is a luxury I couldn't afford. It makes people nervous. It makes them see you as dangerous instead of reasonable. And reasonable was the only door you left open.

I don't say that as criticism. I say it as fact.

You believed the law could protect me if we argued carefully enough. I never believed that. What I believed was that you could make them write it down.

And you did.

Everything they did to me – the arrests, the delays, the permits that vanished, the work that dried up – all of it happened while the law watched.

That's not failure. That's evidence.

Maybe not for my case. Maybe not in my lifetime.

But someone will read that transcript. Someone will see the pattern. Someday they will say: "This is what the law permitted."

And they'll have proof.

You gave me that.

You also asked – more than once – if I regretted filing. If the cost was worth it.

Here's my answer:

The question is wrong.

It wasn't about worth. It was about refusal.

I refused to disappear quietly. I refused to let them keep calling it order when it was violence. I refused to let my children grow up believing compliance would save them.

You made that refusal matter.

Not by winning, but by recording.

If I have one regret, it's this: I wish I'd told you sooner that the restraint you thought was protecting me was really protecting them.

The system doesn't change because we ask it nicely. It changes because people make it too expensive to stay the same.

And expense isn't always money.

Sometimes it's dignity. Sometimes it's silence. Sometimes it's the refusal to pretend that procedural fairness means anything when the procedure itself is the weapon.

You'll teach again. I know you will. You're too curious about the law to leave it alone.

When you do, teach them this:

The law worked on me exactly as designed.

Every rule was followed, every procedure was honored, and every decision was defensible.

And I still died carrying it.

Don't let them think that's a tragedy. It's a function.

Teach them to see it. Then teach them to break it.

Helen will be fine. She's stronger than either of us. The children will grow up knowing I tried. That's all any of us get.

But you – you're the one who has to live with what you learned.

Don't waste it on guilt. Use it to become the kind of lawyer I needed before I met you.

The kind who doesn't wait for the system's permission to be right.

– Henry

Silas folded the letter, his hands shaking.

"I didn't know," Silas said finally. "I didn't know what the restraint was costing him."

"Yes, you did," Helen said quietly. "You just didn't let yourself believe it mattered more than the strategy."

The words should have been cruel. They weren't. They were just true.

"What do I do with this?" Silas asked, not meaning the letter. Meaning everything.

Helen considered him respectfully.

"You teach," she said. "Like he told you to."

"I don't know if I can."

"You will," Helen said. "Because now you know what it costs to be too cautious."

She turned to leave, then stopped.

"Mr. Thorn ... one more thing."

"Yes?"

"Thank you for staying. Even when you didn't understand what you were staying for."

She walked back toward the church, where her children waited.

Silas stood alone in the parking lot, holding a dead man's final lesson, understanding firmly that some debts couldn't be paid, only carried forward.

THIRTY-SIX
University of Memphis

The letter from the law school had arrived three weeks earlier. He left it unopened on the edge of his desk, where it quietly joined the other remnants of his days. He had told himself he would respond when the moment felt right. It never did.

Now, he picked it up.

The envelope felt heavier than necessary. Inside, he found forms, instructions, and a typed note that made no effort to persuade. The language was measured – speaking of teaching, contribution, and the worth of field experience. There was nothing about escape. No hint of redemption. No suggestion that anything lost might be recovered.

Silas read it, then set it aside.

The thought that followed slowly building momentum: Perhaps I could do something there. Not mend, not restore — something quieter and less grand. The law school was small and unassuming. Its hallways, the brochure said, were narrow enough to keep students close. The classes were intimate, names not so easily forgotten. What once seemed a confinement now felt exact and necessary.

He imagined an office with fewer files, a classroom where chairs faced one another instead of a judge's bench. A place where the law was still sharp and dangerous, but open to view from every side — not wielded as a weapon, but studied for what it was.

There was no moment of clarity — just a quiet settling, the kind that comes after the water has been disturbed too many times to ever be clear again.

He gathered his coat, briefcase, and headed home.

Once there, he didn't turn on the radio because Lorraine had already gone to bed, one of her red ribbons left on the table.

He draped his coat over the chair and washed his hands, watching the water bead and vanish. The mirror reflected a man older than he felt, yet more rested than he deserved. He dried his hands and sat at the small desk by the window, where the acceptance form waited to be made official.

He filled it out with care, signing his name as he always had — plain and unadorned. He dated it precisely.

When he finished, he didn't read it again.

He slipped the form into the envelope and sealed it, the sound final. He placed it by the door to remember it in the morning.

That night, he dreamed of a classroom.

There was no lecture. The students were already seated when he entered. No one looked up. They were reading, or waiting, or lost in thought. The room didn't demand his authority — only that he be present.

When he woke, the house was quiet.

He got Lorraine's enthusiastic blessing after a brief discussion. She had been asking to leave the area for a while. He took the envelope with him as he left.

The air outside was cool, sharpening the edges of the morning. He walked to the mailbox, pausing with the letter in his hand before letting it go, then raised the flag.

As he turned toward the office, he felt the old urge to look back to the mailbox – to check, to measure, to account – but resisted. Some actions do not require witnesses, not even one.

Within days, his desk was empty.

He sat there, hands resting where paper had been, waiting for the familiar feelings: relief, sorrow, or forgiveness. None came. What stayed instead was quieter, more lasting.

For the first time since Henry's death, the sense that something had finally stopped ending.

Nuremberg, Mississippi

THIRTY-SEVEN
Packing Day

His assistant, Mrs. Bladen, arrived late in the afternoon, apologetic though there was nothing left to apologize for. She had already packed most of the books the week before, packing up his files with a care that bordered on tenderness.

They worked side by side, their movements quiet and practiced, the kind of shared routine that needed no words. She labeled the final box in her precise script and nudged it toward him.

"I wanted to tell you in person," she said, her voice low, almost casual. He already understood.

Robert Bullock had made her an offer. The firm was growing — busy, steady, and certain in ways that suggested a future. Much of the business, Silas realized, had shifted from his hands to theirs, yet that knowledge brought no bitterness. Instead, it rested with the soft weight of an ending completed, the sense that the circle had come full.

"I start next week," she told him. "They're good people."

"I know," Silas replied, and he did.

She hesitated for a moment before moving closer to hug him. The embrace was fleeting and awkward, but wholly sincere.

"I'll miss this," she said, meaning the quiet partnership, not the work itself.

"So will I," Silas answered.

They lingered briefly, neither in a rush nor eager to mark an end to what had passed. He was grateful for her loyalty and sacrifices, and because he knew she would move forward, never requiring explanations or apologies.

After her departure, the office felt calmer. It wasn't lonely or vacant, simply at peace.

As the last of the office was being packed away, he found a dusty, unopened letter under his desk. The return address was Washington, D.C. There was no name.

U.S. Department of Justice – Civil Rights Division

PRELIMINARY CASE INTAKE – INTERNAL REVIEW ONLY

Case Reference: Logan v. Mississippi
Source of Referral: Informal transcript review (State proceedings)
Prepared By: Intake Analyst, Civil Rights Division
Date: February 28, 1969

Summary:

Transcript review indicates a departure from routine state-level adjudication into matters potentially implicating systemic enforcement practices.

Plaintiff counsel argument, while framed as contextual rather than accusatory, describes a pattern of exclusion and discretionary enforcement not codified in statute but allegedly administered through coordinated silence and delay. These remarks were allowed to stand in the record without limitation or instruction to strike.

Of note:
– Counsel explicitly referenced judicial behavior without naming individual judges.
– The presiding judge didn't intervene to narrow scope.
– The State's objection lacked specificity and was denied.
– A subsequent request for recess was also denied.

This sequence suggests either loss of courtroom control or deliberate tolerance.

Assessment:

At present, the case does not present a clean vehicle for immediate federal action. No explicit constitutional claim was adjudicated at this stage. However, the transcript establishes language, framing, and factual predicates that could support broader inquiry if corroborated.

The value of the case may lie less in outcome than in record formation.

Recommendation:
1. Flag transcript for continued monitoring.
2. Cross-reference counsel's descriptions with existing DOJ files concerning sundown practices in the region.
3. Revisit intake posture if State proceedings escalate or if similar language appears in subsequent cases.

Analyst's Note (Not for Circulation):

There is nothing incendiary here.

The argument reads as if it were written for later citation.

Someone knew this would not end in that courtroom.

THIRTY-EIGHT
The Unnamed Tree

Helen had arranged the table before Silas got there, but there was nothing ceremonial about the act. She simply cleared away the clutter and laid out what was needed, giving space for words neither of them wanted to say. When Silas came in, Helen was already seated, her fingers resting quietly on the wood, her attention sharp and steady.

Silas sat across from her, not waiting for an invitation. Helen's question arrived without warning: "What do you do with the file now?" It caught him in a different way than he'd been bracing for.

After considering, Silas answered, "It's closed. Officially." Helen accepted this with a small nod, unperturbed. "And the documents?" she pressed. "They're in my care," he said, uncertain in tone.

She considered the information carefully, her expression reflecting thoughtful deliberation. "Henry believed the paperwork mattered, even if no one else did."

He didn't try to justify himself.

Helen went on: "Success didn't matter to him. He valued what these papers required – a person willing to be present." Her statement lingered quietly.

She slid a folded sheet across the table. Silas recognized the handwriting. It wasn't a letter, but something meant to be held onto.

"He wanted them kept," she said, "not lost, and not buried."

Silas read the page slowly. It offered no answers, only its presence.

"I'll keep them," he said softly. Helen nodded, stood up, and turned to the window as life outside went on, indifferent to their sorrow.

"They wrote about him," Helen said. "They called him persistent, like it was a nuisance."

Silas didn't reply.

"He knew they'd say that. What mattered was his name was written." Her expression remained composed, showing neither criticism nor consolation.

"You stayed," she said.

Silas acknowledged the statement, fully aware of its significance.

"That mattered to him, even when it wasn't easy."

Silas gently folded the paper, making sure its original shape stayed intact.

"I couldn't protect him," Silas said, surprised by how factual it sounded.

Helen was silent before replying, "No, you couldn't." There was nothing more to say.

Helen collected the rest of the papers, binding them gently with a paper clip. "Just don't let them be forgotten," she said. "That's all."

When Silas left, he hugged Helen – a first since the day the verdict was read, six years before.

On the drive, thoughts of Henry lingered. Their final moments together were vivid, but goodbye had never come.

Silas drove with no clear plan, following vague directions until the roads narrowed and familiar places faded away. He stopped where the quiet felt right, more by feel than by certainty.

There was a tree by the roadside, striking for its presence more than its location. Its thick trunk bore the marks of time and human contact – a low branch missing, the scar now smoothed over. Silas hesitated, drawn to the tree's bark but decided against touching it, mindful that his actions might be misunderstood.

He stood at a distance, noting the trunk's imperfections, refusing to name them. What couldn't be proven needed no defense.

No plaque marked the spot. The ground was undisturbed, unkept, grass growing.

Lost in thought, Silas reflected on what counted as evidence – how context and interpretation shaped reality, and how this place resisted such efforts. To record it would be to make it something it should not be.

The tree had been a place of suffering, yet it persisted, indifferent to its own history.

Nearby, the road curved gently, forcing cars to slow before speeding up again. The bend seemed to teach people how to observe from a distance, how to see without stopping. Silas found himself comforted by that unspoken lesson.

Reports placed Henry's death at another location, with exact times and coordinates. Records would never tie this tree to the event. Yet Silas sensed a connection that defied official separation. Some truths didn't care about geography.

He stayed longer than intended, subconsciously adopting his courtroom stance as if expecting testimony to finish.

Eventually, he returned to his car, leaving the moment unmarked.

Nuremberg, Mississippi

As Silas drove away, the road signs faded from his memory, unfamiliar and unimportant.

Later, at home, Silas set his briefcase by the door and left it untouched, pretending the contents could remain unopened.

THIRTY-NINE
Cataloging

Silas followed directions and eventually found his new office as a law school instructor. Memphis seemed like as good a place as any to start over.

His key resisted briefly, before turning. The door opened into a room with fresh paint and new carpet.

A temporary placard bearing his name was taped to the inside of the doorframe. It sat slightly off-center. He noticed and let it be.

He carried the boxes in one at a time. They were similar in size, though not in weight. One rested at a slight angle on the floor.

The office was spare but serviceable: desk, chair, shelves. The window faced east. The blinds were half raised and uneven. The morning light entered unobstructed.

He opened the smallest box first. Inside were the books.

The Complete Works of James Baldwin. The set was heavier than it appeared, the spines worn unevenly, one volume more handled than the others. They didn't look curated. They looked used.

They had belonged to Henry.

Helen had given them to Silas quietly, without strings or explanation. He had accepted them the same way.

He placed the books on the shelf, spacing them according to the shelf rather than the set. One leaned forward slightly. He adjusted it, then stopped short of perfect alignment.

From the same box he removed a small frame wrapped in a towel. He unfolded the cloth and set it aside. The family photograph was recent – vacation recent. Blue waves danced in the background. His wife, Lorraine, and their son, Joseph Silas, stood beside him, smiling easily. Dad stood close, less rehearsed, but unmistakably present in the moment.

The frame bore a faint scratch near the bottom edge. He brushed it with his thumb and set the photograph on the desk, angled slightly toward the chair. The angle hid it from casual visitors.

He sat and adjusted the chair until it reached his preferred height. Outside, a door closed down the hall. Voices passed and faded. The new and returning law students would arrive within days.

Silas flipped open a legal pad and neatly wrote his name across the top. Next, he jotted down the course title. After a thoughtful pause, he crossed out one word and replaced it with a more accurate choice. Finally, he included the semester dates, making sure they were correct.

When he finished, he capped the pen and placed it beside the pad.

The books remained where he had set them. The photograph caught the light briefly, then settled into shadow.

Silas took off his jacket and hung it on the hook behind the door. He closed the door gently and returned to the chair.

He sat, hands resting on the desk, and waited for the day to begin.

***

A knock came.

He stood and opened the door to find a woman holding a clipboard, already mid-sentence, as though the conversation had begun elsewhere. She quickly apologized and asked whether he preferred printed campus mail or interagency delivery for faculty notices. There was a form and a pen attached by a thin chain.

"Either is fine," Silas said.

She checked a box, thanked him, and moved on. The exchange lasted less than a minute. When he closed the door, the room was silent again.

Then another knock came. It was the same woman.

"I'm so sorry," she offered. "We received this letter for you a couple of weeks ago and held onto it until you arrived on campus."

"No problem at all," he reassured her. "I've been looking forward to this."

The letter began politely, as these things always did.

Dear Professor Thorn:

The title still felt provisional, like a courtesy extended too early.

The publisher thanked him for his submission. A committee had reviewed the manuscript, and several readers had noted its precision. One had remarked on its restraint. Another had written – almost admiringly – that the work refused the comforts of moral distance.

Silas read that sentence twice, unsure whether it was praise.

Then the letter turned.

The committee, it explained, had reservations about the working title. *Procedural Neutrality in the American South* was accurate, they conceded, but insufficient. It suggested abstraction where the manuscript insisted on consequence. It softened what the evidence had rendered unavoidable.

They proposed an alternative.

The words appeared centered on the page, set apart from the paragraph like a finding of fact:

Nuremberg, Mississippi

The comparison was not, the editor assured him, meant to provoke. It was not metaphorical. It was technical. The manuscript documented a legal system operating within its own rules, staffed by professionals acting in good faith, producing outcomes that were nonetheless consistent, foreseeable, and destructive. The title, they argued, didn't accuse individuals. It described architecture.

They acknowledged the weight of the reference. They acknowledged the risks. They emphasized that the press would not suggest it lightly.

It was accurate, defensible, and consistent with the record.

Silas set the letter down and looked around the office. This, he thought, was how things became permanent – quietly, under institutional letterhead.

He drafted a response that afternoon.

It was careful. It cited precedent. It warned of misreading. It suggested alternatives that preserved severity without inviting unnecessary attention. He argued that the work spoke for itself. That the facts were sufficient. That titles had a way of becoming shortcuts.

He didn't send it, instead he threw it in his briefcase and went home.

That night, Lorraine asked him how the office setup was coming along.

"Fine," he said.

He slept poorly.

In the morning, he removed the letter and read it one more time. This time, he didn't linger on the justifications. He looked only at the title.

It was not wrong.

He took out a clean sheet of paper and wrote a single word:

Proceed.

He signed his name in blue ink.

When he returned the letter to the envelope, he noticed – only then – that the publisher had included a second page he had not read. A permission form with cataloging information.

At the bottom, already filled in, was the line that would eventually follow his name in libraries he would never visit.

Nuremberg, Mississippi

Nuremberg, Mississippi

FORTY
Logan Scholarship

The letter was forwarded to the Thorns' new address the same week the moving vans arrived.

National Association for the Advancement of Colored People
Mississippi State Conference
Jackson, Mississippi

Dear Mr. Thorn,

The Mississippi State Conference of the NAACP has voted to confer upon you the **Henry Logan–Silas Thorn Justice Citation**, in recognition of your representation in *Logan v. Mississippi* and for professional conduct reflecting adherence to constitutional principle under adverse conditions.

Nuremberg, Mississippi

This citation includes a monetary award in the amount of **$7,500**, intended to acknowledge the personal and professional costs associated with sustained civil rights litigation within the State of Mississippi.

The Conference recognizes that the litigation in question didn't result in the relief sought. Nonetheless, the Executive Committee determined that the manner in which the case was prosecuted – particularly your emphasis on procedural integrity and equal protection – warrants formal recognition.

A brief presentation will be held following the Conference's spring meeting. Attendance is optional. No remarks are required.

Please indicate acceptance by returning the enclosed form.

Respectfully,
Julian Williams
Legal Affairs Chair
Mississippi State Conference, NAACP

Enclosure: Acceptance Form

Without a second thought, Silas knew how he'd use the money.

He sat alone at the small table in his study. The house was silent in a way that encouraged contemplation.

The scholarship paperwork was thin – three pages with carbon copies beneath. He had read them twice already. The language was specific, careful not to promise more than it could guarantee.

The Henry Logan Memorial Scholarship.

To be administered by the University of Mississippi School of Law.

Purpose: To support Mississippi students pursuing legal education with an expressed commitment to civil rights, public-interest advocacy, or constitutional litigation.

Award: Annual stipend for educational materials and fees. Preference given to applicants intending to practice law in the State of Mississippi.

Silas paused at the name.

It had taken longer than it should have to convince the committee to include it. Someone had suggested *The Logan-Thorn Fellowship*. Someone else had suggested *Justice Scholarship*.

Silas had said no and had been surprised when no one argued.

He signed his name slowly, aware that this was the cleanest legal act he had performed since Henry died. No opposing counsel. No objections. No judge pretending not to see what was in front of him.

He signed in blue ink as proof of an original signature.

He stacked the papers, clipped them together, and slid them into the envelope.

The law would train them better than it had protected Henry. Silas understood that clearly.

He sealed the envelope anyway.

The check was waiting in the student mailbox, also signed in blue ink.

HENRY LOGAN MEMORIAL SCHOLARSHIP
Amount: $1,200

The student stood there, reading the name again. Logan. He had heard it before, though not in class. Not in doctrine.

He asked the clerk.

"Oh," she said, thinking. "That was an old civil rights case. '60s, I think. Federal court. Didn't go anywhere."

She shrugged – not dismissive, just factual.

That night, the student found the case in the archive room. Thin file. Fewer pages than he expected. No photograph. No personal history. Just arguments, rulings, and denials.

He noticed the attorney's name.

Silas Thorn.

The opinion ended the way they often did – with restraint, with balance, with the law still intact.

The student closed the folder.

For the first time, he understood something his professors never said aloud: that the law remembers outcomes, not people, unless someone forces it to do otherwise.

The check paid for his books that semester.

FORTY-ONE
Office Hours

The first students arrived early. In his 15 years as a professor, he saw the pattern played out annually. First-year law students were annoyingly enthusiastic. It's also what he enjoyed most about his work.

They waited in the hallway rather than knocking, voices low with papers held flat against their chests as though they were being graded on posture. Silas watched them through the narrow pane of glass in the door. He recognized the attitude – anxious preparedness.

He checked his watch. There were seven minutes remaining.

When the time came, he opened the door and stepped aside. No announcement. No invitation beyond the open space itself.

They entered in single file and chose seats, filling up the back row first, then taking random chairs. One student sat, stood again, then sat farther back. Another placed a notebook on the desk nearest Silas and then withdrew it, uncertain what counted as permission.

Silas waited until they had finished arranging themselves.

"This is not a lecture," he said. "If it becomes one, stop me."

A few smiles appeared and disappeared just as quickly. Pens hovered in naïve anticipation.

He wrote the course title on the board without underlining it. The chalk snapped midway through the final word. He replaced it and continued.

"This course concerns legal structure," he said. "Not belief. Not intention. Structure."

A student in the second row raised her hand halfway, then lowered it.

Silas noticed. He didn't call on her yet.

"In this room," he continued, "you will be asked to defend positions you do not hold and to critique outcomes you agree with. If that troubles you, it is not a flaw. It is material."

He stepped back from the board. The chalk dust remained on his fingers.

Another hand rose, this one fully.

"Yes," he said.

The question focused on procedure – grading, expectations, and whether participation referred to how often someone spoke or the quality of their contributions. Silas gave a concise, direct answer without adding extra details. After he finished, he waited briefly for any further questions, but no one responded.

He glanced at the roster on his desk, then closed it.

"We will begin next week with cases that appear settled. Your task will be to locate what remains active inside them."

The students gathered their things more quietly than they had arrived. One lingered near the door, considering a second question, then thought better of it and left.

When the room was empty again, Silas erased the board. He left a faint outline where the title had been.

He sat, opened his notebook, and wrote the date at the top of the page.

In the hallway, people came and went, creating a noise that ebbed and flowed but never completely stopped.

The knock came later, when the hallway had dispersed and the building had established itself into its afternoon rhythm.

Silas was reviewing a case brief he had already decided would not be assigned. He didn't look up. The knock came again – this time sturdier.

"Yes," he said.

The student entered without waiting for further instruction. He was tall, smartly dressed in a bow tie and loafers, carrying a legal notepad. He closed the door behind him.

"You said to stop you if it became a lecture," the student said.

Silas gestured to the chair across from the desk. "Have a seat."

The student didn't sit right away. He placed the pad on the desk, then took the seat.

"My concern," the student said, "is that the premise of the course assumes instability where the law has already resolved the matter."

Silas folded his arms. "Go on."

"In several of the cases listed," the student continued, "the outcomes are settled precedent. Reopening them isn't analysis – it's revisionism. It suggests the system failed when, in fact, it functioned."

Silas crossed his arms and waited.

The student shifted slightly, encouraged by the silence. "There's a difference between injustice and dissatisfaction. Courts can't correct the latter without undermining legitimacy."

"That's true," Silas said.

The student blinked. "Then why…"

"…why examine them at all?" Silas finished. "Because legitimacy is not the same thing as correctness."

The student leaned forward. "But if a decision has survived appeal, review, and time, then by definition …"

"…it has survived," Silas said. "Not proven."

The student frowned. "That's a semantic distinction."

Silas reached for the notepad and slid it back toward the student. "No," he said. "It's an operational one."

He stood and walked to the board, writing two words without commentary.

SURVIVAL VALIDITY

Then he stepped aside.

"Systems," Silas said, "are designed to persist. That is their primary strength. And their primary danger."

Now the student crossed his arms. "So, the law is guilty until proven innocent?"

"No," Silas said. "The law is effective until examined."

The student considered this, then shook his head. "That kind of scrutiny invites instability. Courts require finality."

Silas returned to his seat. "So do people."

The student's expression hardened. "With respect, that answer isn't doctrinal."

Silas looked him right in the eye. "Neither is yours."

Silence stretched.

Silas opened the desk drawer and removed a single sheet of paper but didn't hand it over.

"Tell me," he said, "at what point does a legal outcome become immune from moral inquiry?"

The student hesitated. "That's not…"

"…a rhetorical question," Silas said. "It's the course."

The student exhaled slowly. "If courts are perpetual suspects, then authority collapses."

Silas nodded. "If authority is never suspect, it hardens."

They sat with that.

After a moment, the student stood. He gathered his notepad, less carefully this time. "I don't agree with your framing."

Silas lifted his head. "Good."

The student hesitated at the door. "Will disagreement affect my evaluation?"

"No," Silas replied. "Just avoidance."

The student opened the door and left it open behind him.

Silas rose and closed it gently.

He returned to the board and erased the two words.

Another student arrived early for his scheduled office visit near the end of the day.

Silas noticed him because he waited so patiently.

Not outside the door, not leaning against the wall, just standing a few steps back from the office, reading a case packet without appearing to read it. When Silas finished writing a note and looked up, the student was already there, hand raised halfway, unsure whether to knock or speak.

"Come in."

The student entered and closed the door carefully behind him.

"I had a question about the syllabus," he said.

Silas gestured to the chair. The student sat, setting his papers on his lap rather than the desk. He didn't rush.

"Yes?"

"In Week Four," the student began, "we're assigned a district court case that never reached the appeals phase. There's no published opinion. I'm trying to understand what we're meant to analyze."

Silas glanced at the syllabus. "Which case?"

The student hesitated – not long, but long enough to register. "Logan v. Mississippi."

Silas looked back up.

The student's expression didn't change. He had not asked the question for effect. It was not a test. Just a request for orientation.

"That case," Silas said, "ended before the court was required to explain itself."

"Yes," the student said. "So, what survives is procedure?"

"And consequence."

The student absorbed that. "I was wondering how far we're expected to go beyond the record."

Silas placed his hands together, refraining from posing the question that had, in effect, already been resolved.

"Your name?" he asked.

"Daniel," the student replied.

"Daniel," Silas said, "you're not expected to go beyond the record. But you are allowed to notice what the record avoids."

He considered this. "Including people?"

"Yes," Silas said. "Especially people."

The student nodded. He gathered his papers, then paused. "For what it's worth," he said, "my father used to say that cases don't end. They just stop moving."

"That's a fair working definition," he said finally.

Daniel stood. At the door, he hesitated again. "Thank you, Professor."

"You're welcome."

After the door closed, Silas remained seated.

He didn't open the drawer where the roster lay.

He wrote one word in the margin of his notes and then crossed it out.

Outside, the hallway lights dimmed automatically, one section at a time.

Silas remained in his office before heading home for the evening.

Nuremberg, Mississippi

FORTY-TWO
Beyond Remedy

After more than a decade of teaching *Logan v. Mississippi,* Silas no longer needed to consult his notes. The sequence was now part of him: motion, response, holding, remand. Repetition had softened the language of the opinion and made it familiar.

He began where he always did – jurisdiction, standard of review, and the court's reluctance to disturb local discretion absent clear constitutional violation. He spoke carefully, yet professionally.

Students listened the way they always did when a case arrived already settled, sitting up and diligently writing.

When a hand rose, Silas acknowledged him without making eye contact.

He looked down at the class roster and noticed the student's name. It was the same "Daniel" who had visited during office hours. For the first time, Silas noticed his full name.

Logan, Daniel. First-year law student expected graduation in 1988.

"Professor Thorn," the student said, "when the court refers to reasonable restraint, is that a factual finding or a presumption?"

Silas hesitated at the question. It was precise, cautious in how it was asked.

"A presumption," Silas said. "One grounded in institutional competence."

The student wrote this down, then looked up again.

"And if the presumption holds," he asked, "does the court still examine proportional impact?"

Every student was looking up now.

Silas responded in a composed and measured manner. "Only to the extent that the impact establishes a pattern sufficient to overcome that presumption."

Daniel asked, "Did anyone discuss if the plaintiff could endure that process?"

The room adjusted in a roomful of ways. A courtroom drama was rising in a 101-law course.

Silas waited a beat too long before answering.

"The court does not assess endurance."

There was the final assessment – clean and accurate.

The student closed his notebook and began rubbing his hands together in a way that Silas had seen before. Henry used to do it when waiting out things he couldn't change.

After class, Silas noticed him standing near the window, looking at his reflection in the glass. He waited until the room emptied.

"My father was Henry Logan," the student said with a sniffle.

Silas walked over and placed his arm across Daniel's shoulder. They hadn't seen each other in nearly twenty years.

"I've read the opinion so many times I almost have it memorized," Daniel continued through stifled sobs. "I understand the reasoning. I understand why the court avoided broader language."

He held a thin copy of the case, well-worn after repeated interactions.

He hesitated, deciding which words matched the moment.

"What I don't understand," Daniel said, "is whether anyone ever asked how long he could hold up under it."

Silas felt, briefly, the instinct to explain. To locate himself inside the constraints of that era.

He did none of that.

"The law worked," Daniel said, offering Silas a way out. "It did exactly what it said it would do."

He gathered his books and headed toward the exit, before looking back.

"It just required more of him than he had left."

The door closed softly behind him.

Silas remained at the lectern. He didn't open the casebook, and he didn't move to erase the board.

For the first time, he saw the case as finished. No solution was reached. He realized that whatever had been lost was gone for good.

Meet the Author

Melvin E. Edwards is an author, journalist, and podcaster whose work examines storytelling as a force of inheritance, conscience, and moral responsibility in American life. Raised in Texas with family roots deep enough to earn membership as one of the first African Americans in the Sons of the Republic of Texas, he draws on Southern history and institutional tradition to explore how injustice often endures through lawful procedure and measured restraint, not violence.

He is the creator and host of the podcast Stories from Real Life and the award-winning author of The Eyes of Texans *and* The Strength of a Thousand Sons. *His debut novel,* Nuremberg, Mississippi, *blends legal drama and literary fiction to examine the space between legality and justice.*

A former newspaper columnist, Edwards has received more than twenty writing honors and additional awards for his published books. In 2026, he was named Male Podcast Host of the Year by the American Writing Awards.

He studied journalism at John Brown University in a former sundown town in Arkansas.

Edwards lives in Texas, where history remains open and unfinished.

CONTACT INFORMATION:

You can reach out to the author or publisher at Contact@mediawelldonellc.com or MediaWellDoneLLC.com.

About the Publisher: Media Well Done, LLC

Media Well Done, LLC is an independent publishing imprint and storytelling company founded in Texas. We publish literary fiction and historically grounded nonfiction that examines the intersection of law, culture, race, and the human experience – stories that demand to be told with rigor, care, and narrative precision.

Our editorial mission is simple: we publish work that illuminates what official histories leave out. We are particularly committed to voices and subjects that have been overlooked by mainstream publishing, and to books built to last.

The imprint operates alongside our flagship podcast, Stories from Real Life – more than 200 episodes of narrative journalism and conversation examining overlooked histories and compelling personal accounts. Named 2026 Best Male Hosted Podcast by the American Writing Awards, Stories from Real Life serves as both a platform and a proving ground for the storytelling values that define everything Media Well Done publishes.

For acquisition inquiries, rights information, or review copies, contact: MediaWellDoneLLC.com.

9 781807 642686